A
Swan's Sweet Song

by

J. Arlene Culiner

A Swan's Sweet Song

Cover Art by *Kim Mendoza*

The Wild Rose Press, Inc.
PO Box 708
Adams Basin, NY 14410-0708
Visit us at www.thewildrosepress.com

Publishing History
First *Last Rose of Summer* Edition, 2015
Print ISBN 978-1-62830-743-6
Digital ISBN 978-1-62830-744-3

Published in the United States of America

He was just the way she'd always imagined a successful playwright *should* be: cool, intelligent, strong, and sexy.

As if aware she'd been watching him, Carston turned slightly, caught her eye. She tried forcing herself to look away. And failed. For an eternity, their gaze held over the space separating them. Then detaching himself from the surrounding group, he headed in her direction.

She commanded herself to pretend indifference, but her pulse accelerated, and her heart thumped a sensual jungle beat. Was this supposed to be pleasure? Something closer to pure panic. She swallowed, tried to summon up some zen-like calm...then realized she didn't have any available. She needed help. Fast.

"Charlie?" she gasped. Looked around. Damn! Where had that man gone now that she needed him? The only thing left to do was run. Except she was incapable of movement. *Fool*. The reprimand didn't get escape muscles into moving order.

Why come over here anyway? What would they talk about? They had nothing, absolutely nothing, in common. She had to stop staring at him like this.

Here he was now, tiny inches away, his jaw a hard definite line, his body that tight, sinewy stretch she'd thought about too many times during the night. But it was the expression in his eyes, warm eyes, humorous eyes, that confirmed her instinct: the immediate, deep reaction was mutual. Try as hard as they could to avoid it, something would happen. It was inevitable.

And for once, she, Sherry Valentine, a woman with a smart answer, a flippant remark for everything, everyone, and every occasion, was tongue-tied.

Praise for J. Arlene Culiner

"Culiner's writing is magnificent, [her] dialogue is magical and masterful. An emotional, heartfelt, dazzling experience."

"...I know who I was when I got up this morning, but I think I must have been changed several times since then."

Alice's Adventures in Wonderland
Lewis Carroll, 1865

Chapter One

He was going on the air with a singer of country music?

How could these people expect Carston Hewlett, mature, well-known urban playwright, to sit with some prepubescent pop star and chitchat about broken hearts or lonesome cowboys? And why the hell had Nick Spring, his New York agent, sent him all the way out here to Midville, to participate in this so-called Culture Festival? Carston decided he'd strangle Nick as soon as he got within pouncing distance of the guy.

The nondescript computer music oozing out of the loudspeaker above his head seemed to emphasize the hopelessness of the situation. He looked around the crowded room and tried to locate Emmanuel Warner, moderator of this impending disaster. There she was, beside the coffee machine. He pushed through the throng until close enough to tap her on the shoulder.

"Emmanuel? I've been waiting here for almost forty minutes now. Why don't we do this interview another time."

"Oh, we can't do that." She had the grace to look apologetic. "But I am terribly sorry about the delay. I don't know what went wrong. Sherry Valentine should have arrived half an hour ago."

"And if we go on the air without Ms. Valentine?" Carston tried not to sound too hopeful. "After all,

1

country music and contemporary theater don't have much in common."

"Don't you like country music?" Emmanuel didn't wait for an answer. "This'll be lots of fun, really it will. People here in Midville just love country music and live theater. Especially the mayor. He'll be on the show too." She threw Carston a dazzling smile to cheer him up.

It didn't work. Sure, she needed to keep her radio guests happy so everything would run like eggs on oiled glass, but he didn't feel conciliatory. He wanted out. Now. He wanted a drink in his hand—a drink with lots of clinking ice—and a big luxurious bed underneath him, all that in the next five minutes. An unattainable dream…

A very nice bed waited for him back at the hotel, of course, and the very thought of it made him miserable. He wasn't anywhere near it. No, he was here, killing time in a room that was getting hotter and noisier by the second and waiting for a country music star. So they could talk entertainment. He needed this like he needed hives.

Emmanuel added a dose of flirtatious warmth to her voice. "Tell me, Carston, what kind of music do you like?"

"Music?" He didn't feel like repartee either. "I prefer the Baroque Period: Bach, Handel, Purcell…although I'd never refuse Britten or Holst."

Her smile faded, and flirtation gave way to astonishment. "Of course you've heard Sherry Valentine's song, 'Raindrops in Winter,' haven't you? It's been at the top of the charts for months."

"No," he muttered with dreary patience. "I've

never heard 'Raindrops in Winter.' " He didn't think he'd missed much either: the title alone made him think of leaky faucets.

"Well, 'Raindrops in Winter' is just a great piece of music. The lyrics are meaningful, and the tune's so catchy everyone's humming it."

He could just imagine. Sarcasm got the better of him. "You weren't, by any chance, planning on me singing a duet with Ms. Cherry Valentine?"

"Sherry. Not Cherry," Emmanuel corrected. Then blinked. "A duet?"

"That's bad enough."

She blinked again. "What's bad enough?"

Carston sighed. *Sherry* Valentine or *Cherry* Valentine: either way the name was so...so saccharine and so fake. But why bother explaining? He didn't need to. A technician across the room signaled to Emmanuel.

"Excuse me..."

Exhausted, he watched her go with relief. All last week, the week preceding the New York opening of his play, had been stress on wheels, and last night's celebration had gone on until five this morning. Then he'd only managed to catch a few hours sleep before setting out on the long drive to Midville, to this Culture Festival.

Country music.

Carston looked over at the entrance—and exit—of the radio station. So near, yet so far. But the wild urge to sneak over to that door, edge out, disappear, avoid the impending ordeal, rolled through his mind. Became an overwhelming need. If he did escape, what could they do? Shoot him?

Probably, he thought with a certain joy. It was

definitely a risk worth taking. Slowly, discreetly, he began crossing the room.

****

Even in the dark, the painted words *Sherry Valentine and Her Boys* gleamed on the side of the bus now rolling down Midville's main street.

"War paint all in place?"

Charlie Bacon's rasping snarl slammed into Sherry's thoughts and sent them scattering. She groaned. Charlie might well be her agent, road manager, and closest friend in the whole world, but he still exasperated her no end when he chucked out those hackneyed phrases and treated her like a twelve-year-old.

"War paint?" She dragged the words out, as if hearing them for the first time.

"You got it, chicken. We'll be at the radio station in less than one minute."

"Cool down, Charlie-boy. This one's a radio program, not live television."

"Got that too." Charlie gummed the smelly cigar Sherry forbade him to light in the bus.

"Well, this'll shock the spurs right off those sneakers of yours: you can't see what people look like on the radio, not even these days, and certainly not in Midville."

Charlie grunted. "So what if the public can't see you. The journalists and the disc jockeys at the station can. And they talk, sweetheart. You don't want them saying you look like something the cat dragged in. Or like a has-been."

"Keep heaping on the flattery," Sherry snapped. "See where it gets you. First stop: the bread line."

Not that Charlie Bacon, top agent, ruthless manipulator, and infamous busybody, ever took offense. Now, he snorted with derision.

"War paint," Sherry muttered. "Contemporary Martian, that's what I call it." She sincerely hated her green contact lenses, dyed orange corkscrew curls, forever-red wet-look lips and clothes so flashy, all and sundry gawked. And pointy cowboy boots made her toes ache.

"You know what the public's like," Charlie continued, imperturbable.

"Boy, do I ever." Her voice took on a high, mocking tone. "That's Sherry Valentine? I never knew she'd be so fat. Or so thin. Or so short. Short? She's too tall. And she's much older than she says she is too. Much, much older. Of course, those boobs can't be hers. I know implants when I see them."

Charlie shook his massive head. "Big deal. It's all publicity for you. Your concert here is sold out as usual, so just give the public what they want. Show your appreciation."

She sighed. "I give the public all I've got all the time. I've given so much for so many years now, I don't even know if I exist when I wake up in the morning."

"Boy oh boy. Look how you're talking. You're the one who wants a new career as an actress. If you think being a singer is rough going, just wait and see what a rat race the film industry is. You'll be wishing for the dull, relaxed days as a country star in no time flat."

"It's possible." Although she hated to agree with Charlie on anything if she could help it. "At least the film world will be a brand new rat race instead of this old familiar one. Besides, if I loathe being an actress, I can pack my bags, go home to Dog's Pass, and marry the boy next door."

"Oh, sure. The boy next door's been married to someone else for the last thirty years."

"Come on, Charlie. Keep in touch with the times. The boy next door has been divorced three times by now. He'll be thrilled to have me knocking on his door."

Charlie snickered, a know-it-all sound. "Fine. Just keep on dreaming. Besides, you're too tough and too much of a rebel to live the easy life. You're also too ambitious to stay home baking cupcakes."

Charlie might be right about all that too, she thought. Unfortunately.

The bus hissed to a halt in front of the brightly lit radio station.

"End of the line, chicken. I'm counting on you. Charm them off their feet."

"Don't I always?" muttered Sherry. She leapt out of the bus and stormed up to the door. She felt as charming as a stoat creeping up on a fluffy bunny.

****

His escape route cut off, Carton's heart sank, descended into a bottomless sea. This gaudy show-business cookie walking into the station had to be the country music singer, no question about it. If she wore twinkling neon lights around her neck, she couldn't have looked flashier. Okay, no young kid…she had to be somewhere around his own age—in her forties? Fifties? Who could tell these days? But take the way she dressed: a red stretch mini-dress displayed every soft inch of her curves and the high white cowboy boots more than emphasized the long slenderness of her legs. Not only that, she'd smeared so much shiny lipstick on her mouth, you couldn't see how finely drawn it was… or you *almost* couldn't see. Clearly she wanted to look as sexy as hell.

Okay, okay. Had to give her credit. She *was* sexy as hell. And aggressive. Certain of her power. He knew the type: a tough, experienced woman who expected men to fall at her feet. Other men. Because his interests excluded banal chitchatting or mindless flirting.

Carston watched the mayor of Midville push his way toward the singer, puff himself up like a rubicund blowfish, and bellow: "Welcome to Midville, Ms. Sherry Valentine!"

As if Rin Tin Tin, Lassie, Queen Elizabeth, and Superwoman all rolled into one had entered the studio, everyone burst into enthusiastic applause. Everyone except himself, of course. He stood aloof, observed the glowing faces around him, and let his resentment build. When *he'd* walked into the station, he'd received nothing more than a few polite handshakes. He, one of the most prolific, brilliantly talented playwrights of the moment (according to *The New York Times*), was considered less important than a country music star. The world had taken a turn for the worse…or in Midville it had. He turned away, headed for the refreshments table, but even here, he couldn't help overhearing the whispered comments Sherry Valentine provoked.

"She's skinnier than I thought," muttered a young female technician.

"Fatter," someone else muttered back. "She even has wrinkles."

"And I know a silicone implant when I see one," said the technician with smug confidence.

Really? Carston forbade himself to turn around again and stare.

"Carston?" Emmanuel Warner stood beside him again. "Why don't you and Sherry get to know each other a little? That way, when we go on the air, our discussion will be smoother, more natural."

He grimaced. Thought about the sort of "natural" conversation you could have with a country music star: chart and audience ratings, fan magazines, business deals, contracts, the ins and outs of the entertainment business. He turned, took another look at Sherry Valentine. Okay, okay. Maybe he was being unjust. Perhaps it was the long legs and glamour that reminded him of screaming fans. Yet her face, well…he had to admit something in her eyes provoked, even danced. Her high, almost austere, cheekbones hinted at discipline, but smile lines around her mouth and eyes indicated humor. So he let Emmanuel lead him, lamb-like, to the slaughter.

He hadn't managed four steps before a heavy fat paw clapped him on the shoulder. Carston fought down a violent wave of hatred: he despised people clapping his shoulder.

A jovial-looking, cigar-chewing individual grinned into his face. "I'll bet you and Sherry have a lot to say to each other, seeing both of you are in the same line of business."

Life looked ugly again. "Line of business?"

"Sure. Entertainment. You know what I mean."

Carston knew, instinctively, this man was tenacious and would never be warned off by a frigid

8

look or icy tone of voice. Still, he had to try. "Being a playwright is not a line of business."

The man ignored him, of course. His fat paw waved in the air to attract the attention of the country music singer. "Come over here, chicken. Come chew the fat with Carston Hewlett. I told him you have a lot to say to each other, both of you being in show business."

Carston caught her wince. Did it mean she had no more desire to "chew fat" with him than he with her? Not that he cared. Still…why didn't she want to talk to him? And why be irked by her indifference?

Without much enthusiasm, she sauntered in his direction and stopped in front of him. Boldly, she let her eyes slide up and down. Carston almost laughed. She was evaluating him, sizing him up like a chunk of roast beef or a steak, calculating how tender he might be. Well, he had nothing to be ashamed of. He had a trim body and easy grace. Women loved his gray eyes, his silvered mahogany hair, and weren't physical attributes a more immediate magnet than intelligence? But this singer giving him the once-over didn't look so pleased about the physique. Or his reputation. Who did she think she was?

He met her eyes with an equal lack of warmth. Ms. Valentine would learn, very quickly, she was out of her depth when it came to him. But even as the thought crossed his mind, he felt his fatigue and pent-up hostility trickling away. To be replaced by interest. And something akin to desire. Desire? How could his body betray him in this way? He struggled to smother the reaction, nip it in its first, traitorous bud. This country singer was a charmer. She knew what effect she had on men. His mind raced, searched for meaningless conversation to smash the powerful silence, quash the sensations and, above all, to hide his reaction from her.

He kept his tone cool. "Hard to understand why we're being interviewed together."

"Just what I thought," she answered, just as icily.

Carston stared harder. Her voice had taken him by surprise: low, vibrant, it clashed with her flashy appearance. Now he really was intrigued. Very much so.

"We *are* on opposite sides of the cultural world." He noted how condescending he sounded. Did it matter? Well, in a way, it did. He had the vague suspicion that condescension might not be the right tactic to take with Sherry Valentine.

A sarcastic smile slid over her beautiful lips. "That's why you were sneaking out the door?"

Her words pulled him up short, shoved soft, sensual thoughts to the back of his mind. So she'd seen what he'd been up to? He felt himself squirm and sensed he had to justify himself for some crazy reason.

He shook his head. "Fatigue. That's why I wanted to get away. What I need right now is a nice big bed with crispy sheets, just like the one waiting in my hotel room. Believe me, I know how good those sheets will feel when they slide over my skin tonight." He stopped, shocked by his own words. Was he crazy? Talking about a bed, sheets, skin? He'd intended to keep the conversation on neutral ground—then had dropped into the trap. Reacted the way all men would. Did Sherry Valentine now expect him to pull out the big guns? Invite her back to that bed of his for a torrid night?

But she ignored the innuendo. Her lips crooked up

into a smile of complicity. "A comfortable bed? Sounds heavenly. Just add a glass of wine and a good book to that picture."

Carston stared. Had she just suggested they crawl into bed together? With a book? She must be having him on. She didn't look like the sort of woman who'd spend her bedtime hours indulging in literature. "You read a lot?" He sounded arrogant again.

Her amiable expression faded, became something warlike. "I actually liked reading *Eye of the Storm*."

He stared at her with astonishment. "You read my play?" Few enough people even went to see live theater these days.

"Oh yes, Mr. Hewlett." Her voice dripped sarcasm. "I can assure you we singers do know how to read." She opened her eyes wide. "Guess what else? Way back when, I even went to school."

He was ashamed of himself. "Sorry. I didn't mean to insult you. It's just that people very rarely read plays."

She observed him thoughtfully for a few seconds. "You weren't by any chance thinking that as a singer of country music, I spend all my time posing for gossip magazines and chewing hay?"

He couldn't deny she'd put her finger on it. He felt like a squirming eel. "I also find my own arrogance intolerable."

Defiance disappeared from her face, was replaced by amusement. He might be out of the eel category now, but before he could confirm it, Carston felt his shoulder clapped by another over-enthusiastic hand.

"Well, folks. How's Midville treating you?" It was the mayor again.

11

Carston sighed. Since arriving in town, some four thousand people had grinned at him and said: "You'll like Midville, Mr. Hewlett. It's a friendly little place."

And then there'd been all those banners strung up across the streets:

Welcome to Midville
The friendliest town this side of the Rockies

Clearly, all the citizens took that message seriously.

The mayor was still leering at them—no, Carston had to revise that thought: *he* was being ignored. The leer was reserved for Sherry Valentine. "Pleased to have you with us for the festival. You'll like Midville. It's a friendly little place." He slapped Carston on the shoulder again before moving off.

Carston watched him malevolently. "Why did I leave my porcupine quill suit at home?"

He heard Sherry laugh, a rich, throaty sound. His heart grew lighter, left the sea of despair, and began floating. Because he'd made a woman called Sherry Valentine laugh? He felt his skin tighten and his muscles expand. Words vanished; ideas disappeared. The reception room, the crowd, the throb of bad music, all receded. He examined her aquiline nose and arching brows.

She stared back at him in the same dazed way, eyes liquid, pupils widening, and he knew they'd both been snagged by a primitive reaction: the call of male to female, female to male.

"Carston? Sherry?" Emmanuel Werner's cooing voice seemed to come from a great distance away. "Let's go. We're on the air in two minutes. But there'll be plenty of time after the show for all of us to get to know each other better."

Carston blinked. Came skiddering back to reality. Slightly embarrassed, he glanced at Sherry, but the sensuality and interest had vanished. Now her expression was neutral.

Chapter Two

The Midville Assembly Hall and Cultural Center had been decorated with colored streamers, exotic plants in plastic, and the inevitable banner:

Welcome to Midville
The friendliest town this side of the Rockies

Carston leaned against a pillar and wondered where the hell Sherry Valentine was, then wondered why the hell he was even wondering. Did it matter? It did, although he couldn't have explained why. Or maybe he could: desire. *Idiot*, he chided himself. He stared around the hall again, scanning every hairstyle, every dress, and every pair of legs. So, she wasn't here. Not yet. A begrudging flash of intuition told him she'd make a late arrival, one calculated to catch eyes. Isn't that what flashy stars did? Of course. Hadn't he seen that yesterday at the radio station?

Only, for some reason, the idea didn't irritate him this evening. No, he thought with surprise. Her entrance could be as dazzling and tardy as she chose. Just as long as she got here.

Last night, after the radio program—a program dull enough to send a stadium of insomniacs into deep sleep—he'd hoped to resume conversation with the intriguing Sherry Valentine. No such luck. Emmanuel Warner had taken his arm and tried to possess him. He'd caught Sherry looking at him with what he'd interpreted as mockery, then could only watch as she and her agent strode out of the station door. Later, alone in his hotel room, Carston hadn't been able to stop thinking about her despite his fatigue. How had she managed to get under his skin like that?

And what did he want from her? All the pleasures a one-night stand could bring? That would spice up the days and nights here at the Culture Festival. But the more he thought about a possible fling, the more he knew he didn't want something so banal: he'd left that stage behind him many years ago. These days, older and wiser, he liked taking his time, getting to know a woman, and finding out what made her tick. Relationships no longer had to do with conquest, with seeing how little time it took before rolling onto a bed together. As for Sherry, well…he still doubted they had much in common, but she'd read his play, and that showed there was an unexpected side to her. He wanted to know more.

Suddenly, he found himself surrounded by a cluster of people. A nervous-looking man announced they were the coordinators of the local drama group.

"How wonderful it is to meet you, Carston Hewlett. To talk to you in person."

"And it will be so exciting to see your play here in Midville," added a woman in a green hat. "Of course, our group doesn't perform your work. It's just a bit too sophisticated for our audience."

Before he could open his mouth to reply, the nervous man intervened. "Although we do put on famous plays. Last year it was Macbeth, and we managed to cut it down to three quarters of an hour, songs and dances included."

Carton's eyes scanned the room again. If Sherry Valentine were standing here beside him, he might even enjoy this sort of conversation. So where the hell was she?

****

A glowing evening sun streaked the sky above suburban Midville. Sherry, the five boys of her band, and Charlie Bacon crossed the parking lot of the Midville Cultural Center, their multi-colored cowboy boots sending gravel spinning. As usual, their fringes shivered, sequins sparkled, and the tight white jeans they all wore were almost iridescent.

"Budget Magnificent Seven," muttered Sherry to no one in particular.

"Just a foretaste of that long and tedious Hollywood career in B films." Charlie smirked.

"Oh, come on," Sherry countered. "This is singing? We're here in Midville to do a concert, right? Not to go to cocktail parties. Yet here we are. On our way to a cocktail party. This is the limit, the absolute limit. I hate cocktail parties."

"I know what you're going to say next too." Charlie nodded complacently. "Know it all by heart. You're going say you're firing me and going back to Dog's Pass to marry the boy next door."

"And live happily ever after," added Sherry while chucking Charlie a look meant to terrify. But he and the five boys only guffawed.

"Once a day."

Sherry didn't look at Charlie. "Once a day what?"

"At least once a day, every day of the year, you mention Dog's Pass and that creep next door. I've been your manager for the last seventeen years, so that makes what? At least 6,205 times I've heard it."

Sherry tried not to laugh. Then stopped walking, stared up at the Cultural Center, an inauspicious building in gray cement. Grimaced. "Now, isn't this a fine example of architecture. Something between a warehouse and a bus depot. Circa 1963. Then they talk about culture?"

"Didn't your mother tell you if you made faces like that, they'd be permanent one day?"

"My mother was too busy falling in love with whichever new male came to town to worry about what her daughter would look like in the old folk's home."

"Then forget about going back to Dog's Pass. I'll bet the guy next door had a family that never did approve of you and yours. And still wouldn't, big star or not."

Sherry grinned sheepishly. "Bingo, Charlie. The kids next door weren't even allowed to breathe the same air I did, much less look at me. I bet the ban's still on."

****

As absorbed as everyone was in chitchat and fake champagne, it still would have been difficult, if not impossible, to miss the arrival of Sherry Valentine and her boys in the Cultural Center.

"Grin, folks. All eyes are on you."

They paused in the entrance, just the way Charlie had trained them to do. Glowed. Even Sherry gave her most dazzling, show business smile: being on stage (to quote Charlie) was a full time job.

Entrance ritual over, Sherry's eyes roved over the crowd. She picked out several familiar faces and had to admit that, despite its geographic distance from anywhere important, Midville had made an effort with the festival. "I see a few jazz musicians I know. And a pianist—but he's into classical."

"Figure we'll see Hewlett, too." said Charlie. "You know. From last night."

Oh yes, she knew, all right. Last night she'd been more than aware of Carston Hewlett's eyes tracking her every move. Clear, unwavering, gray, they'd seemed to caress her and had sent her blood running hot, cold, then hot again. The man had thrown her off her usual confident stride, had pulled in warm, lazy, sensual thoughts—and the mindless gut reactions she didn't want. So what if he possessed an irresistible masculine aura, and that his voice was rich, deep? That his smile was so wonderful, it gave her an incredible jolt? That her fingers had itched with the urge to run themselves through his gray-speckled hair? So what, all of that? Those reactions signaled lust, nothing else.

She'd also seen the speculative looks Emmanuel Werner, the radio announcer, had given him. Hungry looks. And she'd seen the way Emmanuel had monopolized him after the show. Then, just this morning, she'd seen Carston Hewlett in the hotel lobby, although he hadn't noticed her. He'd been too deep in conversation with yet another infatuated female: a journalist. Well, Emmanuel, that journalist, and all the other women on earth could have Carston Hewlett on a plate, salt, pepper, and parsley included. A man like that would have so many women throwing themselves at his feet, he'd never worry about shoe polish. Some women. Not Sherry Valentine. And the last thing she needed was for Charlie Bacon to suspect her attraction. Charlie was such a manipulator; he'd exploit the information in some awful way.

"You notice that moderator drooling over Hewlett last night?" Charlie chuckled with satisfaction.

"Who could have missed it?"

"But he didn't even give her a glance. There was only one woman in the room he had eyes for. You."

"Oh?" She tried to sound vague. *Damn!* So he *had* noticed. From now on, she'd definitely be on shaky ground...although it was very nice indeed, to hear Carston Hewlett's interest in her had been so obvious.

"Yup. He was like a hungry cannibal doing a little pre-lunch dance," Charlie continued inexorably. "Which is good, very good."

Sherry's eyes narrowed with suspicion. "Why good? What are you getting at now?"

He looked chuffed. "Seems to me even a cannibal has to like the meal he's being served before gobbling it up. Stop fretting. Things will work out fine."

Sherry almost hissed. "Things?"

But Charlie was silent: he wouldn't reveal his evil plans this early in the game. Perhaps she could avoid meeting Carston Hewlett again and circumvent disaster. And why worry? She had a concert to do, interviews to give, and contacts to make so her name stayed in the forefront. And when this festival was over, she'd climb back into the bus with Charlie and her boys and ride away. Perhaps head for the new career she'd been dreaming about—because, according to Charlie, there was serious talk of a role in a television series...

Yes, she had enough on her agenda. No room for a temporary fling. A fling at a conference like this? That had become so commonplace, it was positively banal. And, at this stage of her life, it would also be undignified.

"There he is now," said Charlie, ripping into her thoughts. "Right over there. On the left. You see?"

Of course, she saw. How could she miss him? Tall, mighty easy on the eye, he leaned, glass in hand, against a plaster pillar, listening to the dozen people surrounding him.

"Don't make plans," she warned Charlie. Yet she couldn't avoid looking in Carston's direction again and noticed he didn't seem to be enjoying himself. Oh, he nodded politely at what was being said, but his eyes had that vague glazed look that comes just before sinking to the floor with boredom. But didn't he look delicious in that brown silk shirt and elegant tweed jacket; look how those jeans hugged his long legs. He was just the way she'd always imagined a successful playwright *should* be: cool, intelligent, strong, and sexy.

As if aware she'd been watching him, Carston turned slightly, caught her eye. She tried forcing herself to look away. And failed. For an eternity, their gaze held over the space separating them. Then detaching himself from the surrounding group, he headed in her direction.

She commanded herself to pretend indifference, but her pulse accelerated, and her heart thumped a sensual jungle beat. Was this supposed to be pleasure? Something closer to pure panic. She swallowed, tried to summon up some zen-like calm...then realized she didn't have any available. She needed help. Fast.

"Charlie?" she gasped. Looked around. Damn! Where had that man gone now that she needed him? The only thing left to do was run. Except she was incapable of movement. *Fool*. The reprimand didn't get escape muscles into moving order.

Why come over here anyway? What would they talk about? They had nothing, absolutely nothing, in common. She had to stop staring at him like this.

Here he was now, tiny inches away, his jaw a hard definite line, his body that tight, sinewy stretch she'd thought about too many times during the night. But it was the expression in his eyes, warm eyes, humorous eyes, that confirmed her instinct: the immediate, deep reaction was mutual. Try as hard as they could to avoid it, something would happen. It was inevitable.

And for once, she, Sherry Valentine, a woman with a smart answer, a flippant remark for everything, everyone, and every occasion, was tongue-tied.

"Champagne?"

She let out her breath and nodded gratefully. At least he seemed to be able to maintain a certain presence of mind. His eyes traced her mouth, a glance that sent shivers to all parts of her body, before he turned and smoothly, elegantly, strode in the direction of the table laden with Midville's party snacks. When he returned, she took the icy sparkling drink from his hand. Briefly, their fingers met, and a searing purl of electricity shot up her arm and directly into her heart.

This was ridiculous. She wasn't an adolescent with a first crush or a young woman overwhelmed by a potential mating partner. She was supposed to be worldly wise, aloof, and far beyond such hormonal chaos. She had to cut this out. Her body had to cut it out. She felt his gaze play over her again, strong, intense, skimming her cheekbones and tracing her skin, her mouth. A gaze almost tactile.

"Do you know Midville well?" he asked, idly.

At least her stunned mental powers could cope with that one. "Never been here in my life." She smiled up at him, relieved at this unexpected offer of simple, mindless conversation. Silence was dangerous, too strained, too filled with innuendo.

"But you go everywhere on tour with your concerts?"

She nodded, flicked her hand back with a dismissing movement. "Everywhere and all the time. I've spent the last twenty years living on planes, in our bus, and in hotel rooms that all look the same: with white walls, framed pictures painted by computers, and furniture made out of material created by extra-terrestrials. Let's not get onto the subject of plastic road food."

He laughed. "Don't you mind any of that?"

She shrugged. "I guess I don't let myself think about whether I mind or not. What's been important up until now is making sure each concert is as good as it should be."

"Up until now?" He raised his brows questioningly, but the smile still played on his lips.

Damn, he looked wonderful. The strange, deep feelings his presence evoked had caused those few traitorous words to pop out of her mouth. A faint giveaway flush crossed her cheeks, but she certainly wouldn't reveal her acting dreams to an incredibly sexy and very successful playwright. He'd probably think she'd glom onto him for his influence, for a foot in the door, for a casting couch entry into stardom. "What I meant was, I'm at that point in my career where I can afford to slow down a little." She hoped she'd covered her tracks adroitly enough.

His voice was gentle. "And what will you do with the free time?"

It was almost as if he were telepathic. Sherry scraped around in the nooks and crannies of what was left of her mind for something neutral to say. She needn't have bothered. They had been surrounded by a cluster of grinning people.

"Oh, Mr. Hewlett, we're so honored to have such a distinguished playwright here for our little festival," said one woman in a chipboard dress.

Sherry couldn't ignore the regret crossing Carston's face.

"And we've decided to take advantage of your talent. Perhaps you could give us a few tips for this year's children's performance."

A man with many teeth grinned rakishly. "We're hoping to use the fifty Easter bunny costumes left over from the parade."

Was it a joke? Probably. But Carston's expression had changed again, become desperate. Sherry bit her lip so she wouldn't burst into laughter. So this was what being an intellectual playwright was all about? She leaned in closer, said, *sotto voce*, "Want some lyrics for those fluffy bunny songs?"

His shout of laughter sent thrills down her spine. But the woman in the chipboard dress had overheard, and she looked less than amenable. "Our performances provoke intellectual reflection, Ms. Valentine. They're not light entertainment."

Now it was Carston's turn to grin wickedly, but Sherry didn't mind. His mouth was so wonderfully nice when it quirked upward. But why think about his mouth? What was she doing? Drooling over him just like all the other women on the planet. She had to nip this in the bud if she intended to save her skin. She did want to, didn't she? Except…she wasn't quite so sure about that just now.

Saving her skin, staying cool, uninvolved, well, that didn't sound very exciting. But was a quick, temporary fling worth the heartache and the ultimate disillusion that galloped in on its heels? No. It wasn't. Scowling, Sherry half-turned, took a few steps away from Carston and his admirers.

"Someone cart your pet poodle off to the bottling plant?" Charlie Bacon had appeared at her side, surging up from nowhere, handing her another glass of fake champagne.

"Phooey. I'm having a great time, really I am." Sherry shrugged. "I never knew it would be so much fun meeting people I'll never see again in my life."

"What's the matter now? Why the sour grapes? Mr. Ivy League Playwright getting too much attention from the crowd? Your intimate moment gate-crashed?"

"Mr. Ivy League Playwright? Intimate moment?" She was furious—or maybe embarrassed at being caught out. "Wrong, Charlie-boy. Mr. Ivy League Playwright and I have exchanged very few words and much less than a paragraph."

Charlie laughed, a raw, carnivorous sound. "You don't need words, chicken." His eyes shifted into Carston's direction. "What's up? Love knocking at the door? Finally?"

"Love?" Sherry glared. "You've lost your mind, Charlie-boy. Love and show business? The words don't even sound nice when they're together in the same sentence. I know what I'm talking about, and you do too. I'm too old to believe in fairy tales. Been there, done that." And those experiences—two divorces, several other failed relationships—had taught her love was an illusion. A word. Temporary madness. Something that wouldn't last in the real world.

These days, she was too wary and too independent to get emotionally involved with anyone—especially someone also in the public eye. Her reaction to Carston Hewlett had been pure lust, not love. At least, that's what she'd keep telling herself.

"Yup." Charlie looked smug. "Love. It's about time."

"Charlie, cut that out right now." She had to get his snuffling bloodhound's nose off the trail.

"No way. You always tell me to mind my own business, keep my nose out of your affairs, and get on with the job of keeping you rich and famous. Well, that's exactly what I am doing."

"Oh?" She knew Charlie so well. Squatting and ready to pounce in every square inch of his being were sordid ideas about dollars and cents. He'd exploit a fruit fly if he could make that obnoxious insect's career profitable.

"You want to be an actress, right? That's what you hammer into my head every day of the week. You want to go to Hollywood, act in films. You're the one who reads plays all the time; you're the one who pushed me into making contact with Prima Productions."

"And?" She felt her insides squeeze with dread. But first, let Charlie implicate himself. Then she'd counter attack, smash his proposal to smithereens. She knew it had to do with Carston. It *had* to.

"Well, chicken, listen to this." Charlie pulled the

25

habitual, wet cigar out of his mouth—something he only did when about to say something of the greatest importance. "What's better for an actress's reputation than a personal connection with a big shot playwright? What's sweeter than publicity? A few magazine articles linking your names, a few intimate dinners, and there you are. People are talking about you and connecting you with the theater world." His face was sausage red. "Wonderful!"

"Charlie, if you dare, just dare, I'll strangle you. But very slowly and painfully."

"What's wrong with my plan?" He wasn't in the least discouraged.

"What's wrong? A million things. Number one: I want to be an actress on my own merit, and that's easy enough. I have a name, don't forget. That's already publicity."

"Sure you do. You have a name as a country music singer but not as an actress. You won't get exciting roles because of that."

"Two: I don't know Carston Hewlett at all, but I can assure you he comes from another world. Not from ours. The cheap publicity you're thinking about would render him hostile, and the plan would backfire. I know it."

"You finished?"

"Not until I've made myself clear: back off, Charlie Bacon."

Because…what if something, something soft, something delicate…something intense…was about to flower? What if? But when Charlie started his meddling, it would be destroyed. Mercilessly. Show business gossip, show business publicity, those things wreaked hell on personal relationships. She'd seen it happen too many times.

Charlie shrugged, his face expressionless. Sherry watched him with growing anguish. Charlie with a plan was a man obsessed, and neither snow, nor rain, nor gloom of night would stay him from his appointed goal. Perhaps pretending indifference was the best tactic? Or a silly diversion of some kind?

"Guess what, Charlie? Inside information has it there's a surplus of Easter bunny costumes here in Midville. How about a concert in drag?" Had she been a little heavy on the champagne?

Charlie snorted but didn't bat an eyelid. "All depends on the color. The boys look like hell in pink. Find horse costumes and you're on."

"Horses? Did I hear you talking about horses?" A tall and lusty-looking rancher had moved in. Towering over Sherry, his hot eyes traveled, with precision, over her figure in the tight jeans and fringed shirt. He licked his lips in an equine way.

Two seconds later, an older state senator had also appeared and was soon trying to convince Sherry that connecting up would be an excellent idea: just think of the publicity it would generate. Right now, though, he seemed particularly interested in a connection with her left ear lobe.

"We'll spend the day out at my place tomorrow," the rancher insisted. "I'll pick you up at two. Dress for riding, and you'll see the finest countryside this area has to offer. And I own all of it." His leer left little doubt about what he hoped the day's activities really would be.

"I'm terrified of horses," said Sherry. At least that

was true enough.

"If we just slip away," the senator whispered. He was standing so close, if she turned, they'd do mouth-to-mouth respiration. "I know just the place for a very intimate dinner."

"Sounds great, Senator. Charlie Bacon and my boys will be thrilled to bits. They love eating, and they're heavily into intimacy."

"No one could be afraid of horses." The rancher chuckled.

Sherry shook her head with mock sorrow. "Childhood trauma. My uncle once called my aunt an old nag, and she broke his leg with one swing of her left hoof, size ten."

The senator pushed another glass into her hand. "Sexy ears. Anyone ever tell you that?"

"Only male rabbits."

"I raise the best beef cattle this side of the country," the rancher cut in. "Wait until you see the size and quality of the steak I'm going to feed you."

"Sorry. Steak's out. I'm a vegetarian."

The rancher stopped, thrown off his stride for a minute. "You must be joking."

"Absolutely not," Sherry answered soberly. "I believe in animal rights."

"But animals hunt other animals down." The rancher guffawed triumphantly.

"Show me a cow that hunts and I'll eat my hat. Or a steak, if it comes down to it."

"Miss Valentine prefers chewing hay. She confided that to me yesterday evening." The voice, deep and lazy, sliced into the conversation. Carston.

Sherry turned. How long had he been standing

there? Those remarkable gray eyes were dancing. So he'd been watching her and her predicament with open, raw amusement. She felt absolutely blissful.

Taking her elbow, he masterfully led her away from her "fans." There was something so definite in his manner, it stopped the other males from following. *Pure charisma, intellectual cave man style*. Sherry tried to repress a giggle. She had to stop drinking the bubbly stuff.

"Didn't your mother teach you not to talk to creatures with horns and pointy teeth?"

She looked up at him and grinned wholeheartedly. He grinned back just as openly. Her heart did a flip-flop.

"Why, land sakes alive. If it isn't the man who writes bunny plays."

"Are you drunk?" He was laughing at her.

"Passably." The effect of the alcohol she'd consumed was nothing compared to the head-spinning power of his hand on her elbow.

"You need dinner." He led her deftly in the direction of the door, just as if they'd known each other for the last comfortable million years or so. "We're all meeting up at the restaurant."

"Fine. Who's 'we all'? You, me, and those lusty devils back there?"

"Devils don't meet the dress code. Just you, me, Charlie, and your musicians. Charlie said he's reserved a table for us at a place with the unlikely name of The Blue Lagoon."

"Sounds murky," said Sherry, cautiously. It was difficult to quell the niggling little suspicion growing in the back of her mind. Charlie had arranged this? If

Charlie so much as arranged a lady's doily crocheting party, it would be suspect.

"He gave me the address and told me to take you there in my car."

"I see." She looked around quickly. Charlie was nowhere in sight. Nor were the boys. "And just where is darling Charlie right now?"

"He said he was taking your musicians back to the hotel in the bus. He wanted to meet a journalist; they all wanted to make a few phone calls."

"Uh-huh." Her suspicion grew stronger. "All of a sudden, just like that, all the guys got homesick and had to make calls from the hotel? Because their cell phone batteries went dead? Cute."

His eyes searched hers. "Something wrong?"

"No." She shrugged. "Nothing's wrong. Just sounds a little fake, that's all." Actually, it sounded completely fake, but she wasn't going to refuse to go with Carston. No way she'd refuse.

"What sounds fake?"

She shrugged helplessly. "Don't confuse Charlie with the rest of the human race. He's 100% bionic."

Chapter Three

They stepped out into the calm night and Carston led her to a slightly battered, fairly dusty, two-seater sports car, one antiquated enough to be an authentic old-timer.

"I've never been in one of these before," Sherry said as she tried to make herself comfortable. The choice of car didn't really surprise her; it looked like the right one for a writer—even if it was cramped and felt like the ancient springs were trying to work their way up through the seat underneath her.

"No surprise. Cars like this are fairly rare these days. This baby was born in 1960, but I've added a few improvements." He turned, reached across her, and grabbed a seatbelt. At which point she stopped breathing altogether. His mouth was so close to hers. She saw his arm stop in mid-movement. Hesitate. Was he about to kiss her? Her eyelids felt heavy, and her lips swelled. He was so near, and his fragrant warmth surrounded her. A kiss: she knew it would be wonderful.

But he pulled back. The moment was over. She heard the seat belt click into place. His fingers turned the key in the ignition. Her scattered thoughts collided. What had happened? Why had he stopped? She was so certain he'd wanted to kiss her but hadn't let himself. Why?

"Charlie said something about the first intersection, then turn north." Carston sounded perfectly normal as he drove along the road. "Wherever the intersection is..."

"I suppose we could ask one of the locals," she suggested. Her own voice sounded scratchy. Had he noticed? Peering out the car window she saw the streets were deserted.

He shook his head dolefully. "If there were any locals out there they might even be more confused than we are. Everything looks the same. The community center resembles the public swimming pool and the supermarket and the shopping center."

Sherry laughed. "I suppose that's what vernacular architecture is all about."

He laughed too, turned left, turned again. "If only there weren't so many one way streets. How can you go north if you're only allowed east?"

"We could arrive via China." Which sounded not bad as far as the evening's entertainment went. She wasn't feeling in the least hungry. And this was fun.

"We'll find the restaurant eventually, because sooner or later we'll run out of streets. Or roads. Or land."

"Or gas." Which didn't sound like such a bad idea either.

Just so long as they eventually got around to kissing.

****

They finally located The Blue Lagoon on a country lane just outside the town limits. Elegant, dimly lit enough to invite intimacy, it was the sort of place lovers search out when wanting to avoid impertinent stares.

Looks good, thought Carston. How had Charlie managed to come up with an address like this at such short notice? The guy must have feelers stretching all around the country. Still, he couldn't help noticing how wary Sherry looked.

"The rat I thought I smelt earlier stinks to high heaven now," she said grimly.

"Sounds bad as far as dinner goes," he answered lightly.

She stopped looking wary again and, thank goodness, smiled. "I'm only saying this is not the sort of place Charlie Bacon usually drags me and the boys to. Charlie's into cheap eats in huge quantities. Flower arrangements, linen table cloths, pseudo Louis XIV chairs, and lit candles only interest him if they're easy to digest."

"And?"

"I don't think he has the slightest intention of joining us tonight. The whole thing's a plot."

"What sort of plot?"

She didn't answer, but Carston soon saw she'd correctly analyzed the situation. Catching sight of them, the manager bustled over, informed them that Mr. Bacon had left a message: he and the boys couldn't make it for dinner. There had been complications. Carston couldn't be bothered looking disappointed.

Possibly acting on Charlie's orders, they were led to a table that just happened to be in a dark and private corner—but not quite private enough. The busboy took one look at Sherry and flushed a deep, strawberry pink.

"You're Sherry Valentine!" He wriggled like an over-excited puppy. "I'd recognize you anywhere. I collect all your CDs. I'm a big fan of yours."

"Thank you." There wasn't a great amount of enthusiasm in her voice.

Carston cut in deftly. "Cocktail, Sherry?" He'd seen how uncomfortable she was. She hadn't liked being on the receiving end of adulation, and that surprised him. Gave him the feeling that Ms. Valentine would make him re-think a few ideas on light entertainment.

"No more cocktails." Sherry wrinkled her nose. "And never again fake champagne. Some wine would be lovely, though."

When the busboy had taken their wine order, lit the candle on the table, and departed, Sherry shook her head mournfully. "I was sure he'd ask me for my autograph."

"What's wrong with that?" Carston really did want to know.

"It would be nice, just once in a while, to forget the public and become Sherry Human Being. Sherry Human Being going out for an uncomplicated dinner. Of course, according to Charlie, I'm not supposed to think that way."

"Charlie thinks you have to be on stage all the time?" His eyes found her lips again. Again he wondered what they'd taste like. He'd wanted to kiss her in the car. He almost had. Then he'd stopped himself. Pulled back. The movement had cost him quite an effort, but he wanted—needed—to work out what was going on here. Pure desire? Only that? Even so, he wanted to go slowly. Why resemble all those drooling carnosaurs back at the cocktail party?

"I think I have to explain the situation," Sherry was saying. "I want to warn you, because the last thing you need is to get enmeshed in an evil Charlie-Bacon-generated scheme."

"I see," he said. And tried hard not to smile. She wanted him to take her seriously, but who did she think he was? Some kid still wet behind the ears? An innocent who could be tricked into anything?

"Look, Charlie isn't what he seems to be." Her hand flipped backwards, a fine gesture.

The way she moved reminded him of a dancer. Delicate, light. Her fingers were long, her wrists, fragile. He forced his thoughts back to the conversation. "I understand perfectly. He's not your road manager, his name isn't Charlie Bacon, and every full moon, he mutates into something fuzzy?"

Sherry sighed. "Nothing so innocuous, I'm afraid. The fact is, good old nice-guy Charlie isn't so nice. He's the biggest manipulator I've ever met. He treads the narrow line between honesty and dishonesty. He's calculating, and he's a total bully, a steamroller. And fending him off is like trying to convince a dog to share his juicy bone with you."

The busboy was back, pouring their wine and gaping at Sherry.

Carston lifted his glass in a toast, sipped. "I'm impressed."

"Impressed?" Sherry's own glass was still raised. "By the wine?"

"No. By you." He tugged back a smile. "How kind of you to work with someone who's the epitome of evil."

"Okay. Take what I'm saying as a joke. I've done my duty." She put down her wine glass, picked up her fork, and violently stabbed an innocent olive in a dish.

"I just don't see how Charlie could possibly interfere with my life."

"See how naïve you are?"

The waiter appeared. He was older than the busboy, thus was more dignified and not inclined to gape. Sherry told him she was a vegetarian, that anything the cook felt like devising was fine with her: she loved surprises. Carston watched the interaction, saw how her easy smile had the waiter charmed. She obviously had a talent for putting people at their ease and making them like her.

"Is going out to eat a problem when you're vegetarian?" he asked when the waiter had left.

"Usually not. Good chefs usually want to show how original they are. I just put myself in their hands. Look, can we get back to Charlie?"

"Do we have to?" Not that he minded. Any subject of conversation was fine with him. He couldn't believe how much she fascinated him—though he was doing his best to appear calm and collected.

"Look, I love Charlie. For the last seventeen years, he's been my best friend in the whole world. He's also a wonderful agent and road manager, and the boys love him too. But you have to understand how he functions. This dinner, for example, is a pre-arranged publicity stunt. Just that."

"Is it?"

She nodded. "Charlie never had the slightest intention of joining us. He wanted the two of us to be together and alone. No boys. No outsiders. No interference."

What was wrong with that? This was getting better and better. "Why does he want us to be alone?"

She didn't meet his eyes. She even looked embarrassed. It took her a minute before answering. "Because he thinks we'd make a good couple."

Carston felt his repressed smile break its bounds and broaden out into a grin. "Oh, he does, does he?" Well, old Charlie wasn't the only one.

"Yes, but not in the way you think I mean it," she was quick to add. Too quick.

"What way do I think you mean it?" He couldn't even control his voice anymore: it sounded soft, provocative. A couple? The two of them alone? A couple. The word dragged in others: coupling, coupled...

She still wasn't meeting his eyes. "He wants us to be a good couple for publicity's sake. Because he thinks it would be good for my career if people see us together and link us in a romance. Anything. Just so long as I get talked about."

Carston was silent for a few minutes. So? He still couldn't see what the problem was. Why was the linking of his name to hers such a bad thing? Since when was that kind of gossip dangerous? Unless... "Is it really such a terrible idea?"

She seemed astounded by his question. "Of course it is."

"Why? Do you have a serious relationship that could be damaged by the publicity?" He hoped the question sounded light, casual, although the answer was suddenly important to him.

She twirled her glass. Met his eyes steadily. "No."

Ridiculous. He felt like jumping up, clicking his heels together with relief. Why? What possible difference did it make if Sherry Valentine had a million

37

other men in her life? This was a temporary relationship. A good time had by both. A *short* good time. Anything else was impossible. A country music singer with her fans, her publicity stunts, all her flashy glamour, had no place in a solitary writer's life. His intense, almost radical, dislike of crowds and noise certainly had no place in her life either.

She was still watching him. "Do you?"

He blinked. "Do I what?"

"Have any relationship that matters?"

"No." The vulnerability he heard in his own voice astonished him. He tried to cover it up. Sound practical. "Therefore this concerns only the two of us."

She leaned back in her chair. "I suppose so. It's just that..."

Just what? He was getting confused now. What concerned only the two of them? Desire? Desire didn't have scruples. He'd just decided Sherry was a temporary feature in his life, hadn't he? So why take this so seriously? "Doesn't everyone in your world run after publicity?"

She raised a resigned eyebrow. "You wouldn't say that if you knew how damaging the wrong sort of publicity can be."

"It can create a star where there's no talent." Why was he sounding so cynical again?

She didn't take offence. "Of course it can. Well-done publicity can hide bad work, bad music, and bad singing. But your world is just as rotten. Nothing like a good review to hide a bad play or bad acting."

"True."

They watched each other coolly for a minute. The waiter appeared with a dish of mushrooms stuffed with

38

heady spices. The odor wafted temptingly between them.

Sherry closed her eyes briefly and sniffed the air. "Don't those smell heavenly?"

They did. And he loved her enthusiasm, too. Her humor. It would be fun spending time with Sherry—if their schedules allowed that. Which is when the idea came to him...Okay, he was fairly sure he wouldn't like her music when he heard it, but so what? Did it matter? No. He didn't have to live with it or hear it every day.

He leaned across the table. "I'd like to make a suggestion."

Sherry looked at him curiously. "Shoot."

"It might be nice to step into each other's shoes."

She winced. "Believe me, cowboy boots will kill you. They kill me, most of the time. As for spurs, they're hellish."

"I'm serious." But he couldn't stop the grin.

"So am I."

"Let me explain. Here we are, both stuck in Midville for the next few days. Why not take advantage of the time? I could, temporarily, get involved in your world and you in mine. You'll come to my rehearsal, I'll go to yours. You have the advantage because you know what I write, but you'll be starting from scratch if you want to teach me anything about country music."

Her mouth twisted wryly. "Charlie's going to like this, I can tell." Still, she didn't dismiss the idea.

"And you? What do you think?" He held his breath. To him, the plan sounded downright brilliant. It would throw the two of them together and open the door to other dinners for two, tête-à-têtes, intimate moments. Intimacy: that would make the Midville

39

Culture Festival a hell of a lot more interesting than he'd ever imagined.

She reflected for a minute or two, seemed far away, as if seeing another scene altogether. Then came back to the present. Gave him a wonderful smile, one of pure seduction. "Actually, it sounds like fun."

The next time he got anywhere near his agent, Nick Spring, Carston was going to hug that man for getting him involved in the Midville Culture Festival!

****

It was late when they returned to the hotel. The sound of their footsteps echoed along a silent walkway leading between a line of fir trees and up to the front door.

"Sherry?"

She heard the heat in his voice. Stopped. Turned slightly. The tips of his fingers pushed back a lock of hair, caressed her cheek gently. She forced herself to stay right where she was, not throw herself at him or wind her arms around his neck. Where was all her resolution about not having a fling? Would she end up in his bedroom tonight?

Even in the dark, she saw his smile. He knew how she felt.

Then he folded her against him, and she forgot about her scruples. Her arms did slide around his neck; her fingers did tangle in his silky hair. Under all the layers of their clothing, his chest was hard and tight. Curving more closely into his seductive heat, she raised her mouth to his. His lips brushed hers lightly, teasingly. She moaned softly.

"I know," he sighed, his mouth still against hers. "It feels so good."

Her mouth opened, and his kisses became wanting, intense.

Somewhere behind them a car door slammed; Sherry skidded back into reality.

Carston's fingers cupped her face. "Come on. This will be much more fun in private."

Taking her hand in his, he led her up the steps to the hotel entrance. She followed, her body floating, her feet dangling somewhere in the air, and her head spinning.

The glare of the crowded lobby hit her senses with the slam of an electric shock. She felt a million eyes shoot in her direction, in Carston's. Saw the explosion of flashing cameras.

"There she is!" someone screamed. "Sherry Valentine."

There was a roar.

"This certainly makes a playwright's life look dull," she heard Carston say.

But that was just before a dozen journalists and a mass of hysterical fans surged across the lobby floor. They had to get out of there. And fast. "Carston?"

The arm steering her into the open door of the elevator wasn't Carston's. Looking up, she saw Charlie Bacon's shiny face.

And he looked very, very satisfied.

Chapter Four

Gray light filtered through the windows of the hotel's breakfast room, and the hum of early morning conversation mingled with the scrape of knives and forks on china, the clack of spoons.

Sherry, seated at a table with Charlie Bacon and her boys, caught sight of Carston as soon as he appeared. She hadn't exactly been looking out for him. It was more a question of sixth sense. A tingling sensation had told her he was about to walk into the room…then he did. Her heart lurched.

There it was again. The immediate gut feeling. She wished she could order that feeling to stroll over to planet Saturn but knew it was a hopeless undertaking: Carston Hewlett was bane to her, to any woman who wanted to keep sane. She put down her coffee cup knowing the rattling sound was due to her trembling hands. Just look at the state she was in. Because of what? Because Carston Hewlett had kissed her. That was all. All?

Not quite. She'd spent the rest of the night tossing and turning, dreaming about him, about how good his hard, surprisingly muscular body had felt against hers. About the heat and the demand of his mouth. Hell! She just wasn't used to reacting strongly to a man these days. She didn't want to either. Where did he get all those muscles from anyway? Didn't playwrights spend their lives at a desk scribbling or tapping away at computers and getting flabby?

She fought to keep her face expressionless. No need for Charlie and her boys to know that anything untoward was going on, that her thoughts were as scrambled as the yellow mess of eggs on the big plate in the middle of the table.

But now Charlie Bacon had also spotted Carston, although Sherry didn't attribute any sixth sense to him. It was simply that man's beady eagle eye missed nothing, and the wheels of his conniving mind never stopped churning.

"Good morning, Carston," Charlie bellowed out as if the two of them had been best buddies since those prehistoric days when hairy mastodons snacked on ferns, club mosses, and other primeval vegetation. "Come over and join us."

Sherry winced. This was out and out painful. "Charlie, stop it," she snapped. "Maybe the man likes being alone in the morning."

Charlie guffawed. "Why would he want to be alone?" His voice was loud enough to be heard by every other person in the room. Then, mercifully, he stuffed most of a thickly buttered roll into his mouth.

"Perhaps not everyone in the world appreciates your brand of over-zealous socializing at the crack of dawn, Charlie-boy. Some people like to eat their breakfast in peace and quiet."

The desperate plea was unsuccessful. Here was Carston now, standing beside their table, a light smile playing on his lips as his eyes met her own pained ones for a fleeting second.

"Take a seat, Carston." Charlie's voice was still

insistently hearty. Excruciatingly hearty, she thought.

Carston didn't seem to notice—or if he did, seemed not to care. He sat down, contemplated the group with amused eyes, took in their fringed costumes, the green spangled cacti on their black shirts, the sparkling belt buckles and the brightly colored cowboy boots. Two of the musicians wore spurs, and even Charlie Bacon, although he never appeared on stage, sported glittering horses and silvery musical notes on his vast shirt and vest.

"I get the feeling I've just walked into a Hollywood-style rodeo. People don't really ride horses and round up cattle in clothes like those, do they?"

"Cardboard cowboys, that's all we are." Sherry shrugged with what she hoped looked like insouciance or just the usual friendliness doled out to all and sundry.

"Were any of you raised on a ranch?"

Everyone—Sherry, her boys, and Charlie—laughed.

"Nope," said Charlie with a certain raw pleasure. "Don't let word get out, but Todd's a Cincinnati boy, Len's from Miami, Rick hails from Boston, Nat grew up in Toronto, and Jimmy was born in Memphis."

"Suburban Memphis," confirmed Jimmy with a grin.

"These boys are some of the best musicians around, and they've all had formal musical training. Rick Tally, here, can play the meanest violin sonata you've ever heard. Only Sherry has a country background. She was born in the Ozarks."

"In Dog's Pass," added Sherry, quickly. Too quickly? She noted the curious glance Carston threw her way. *Be careful*, she warned herself. *The man has a fine writer's ear. Well tuned, it'll be quick to hear odd notes and small lies.* She looked down at her plate. She was having trouble meeting those calm, amused, gray eyes anyway. "Unlike your actors and actresses who take off their makeup when they leave the stage, we have to play our roles all the time."

"And these words are from the very person who spends most of her time arguing with me about doing just that!" Charlie snorted with derision. "Why, when we were in the bus just the day before yesterday, she was complaining about looking like a Martian."

Sherry ignored him. If she didn't, there'd be no end to the dirty little secrets Charlie would drag out from the complicated swamp of their long partnership. Instead, she kept her voice cool. "You see, back in the twenties and thirties, when Hollywood made the first westerns, authentic country music was mixed together with cowboy music. The result was something called Western Swing. Of course, music has changed a lot since then, but the public wants the lonesome heart-broken cowboy myth to continue."

"Does the slick image ever get mixed up with who you really are underneath?"

"Not if you know what's good for you," grunted Charlie. "If you don't know who you are under all the fringes and makeup, then show business grinds you up in no time."

"Of course, some people do get confused," added Rick Tally. "We had a banjo player on tour with us some years ago: Billy J. Sudds. He was a great musician but a bit on the unstable side. Somehow he got it into his head he'd been reincarnated as Wild Bill Hickok. The real Wild Bill was killed in Deadwood for having cheated at cards, and Billy thought he'd been put back on earth as an avenger."

"I never saw a worse loser in my whole life than Billy J. Sudds." Sherry sighed. "He couldn't even play musical chairs without getting mean."

"In any case, Carston, I guess you can decide for yourself if we mix up real life with show." Charlie was leering and foxy-eyed. "Last night Sherry told me the two of you are going to hang around with each other over the next couple of days, learn a little about each other's business. Sounds like a great idea to me, and I've arranged everything."

"Wait a minute," said Sherry. "Slow down, Charlie, my boy. What's been 'arranged'?" She didn't like the sound of this one bit.

"Keep your hair on, chicken. Why're you so suspicious all the time?" Charlie twisted his face into a perfect example of fake hurt innocence. "You're the one who told me about this plan of Carston's. So why not put it into action right away. Today. This morning. Now."

"No, Charlie. Today I'm going up to the children's hospital. That's not what Carston had in mind."

"Why not go to the hospital together?"

Sherry shook her head. She knew her Charlie; he probably thought she'd tacitly agreed to use Carston to further her acting career—which she very definitely hadn't. She was certain that if Carston got wind of that, he'd never speak to her again. "Carston has better things to do today. I'm sure he has obligations here and…"

Charlie didn't give her a chance to finish. "He doesn't. I spoke to the Mary Scott, the festival director.

He's got the whole day free."

"Charlie, you didn't. Why you horrible, prying—"

"Wait a minute." Carston was actually laughing. "Stop talking about me as if I were a three-year-old in need of a nanny. What's this about a children's hospital?"

"Just one of the things Sherry likes to do when she's on tour somewhere," Charlie roared in before Sherry could even unclench her gritted teeth. "She doesn't do it for publicity, and no journalists are in on it. She thinks it'll bring fun into kids' lives if they get to meet a big star they've seen singing on television."

"I see."

Sherry had to give him a way out. "Look, Carston, I know this isn't what you meant when we talked about accompanying each other, so just ignore what Charlie said. He still treats me like a little kid, and now he's doing the same thing to you."

But Charlie continued on in his usual steamroller way. "Both of you can ride up there in your car, Carston. That'll free me and the bus, so the boys and I can take care of concert arrangements. You know how things are in these backwoods towns: half the time the sound technicians think a plug is something you cut off and chew."

Carston nodded. He was still grinning. "Sounds fine to me."

"Carston, I'm sure you don't want to do this," Sherry pleaded. "Besides, it looks like it's going to start raining any minute now, and the children's hospital is miles and miles away from here." And that meant hours of being alone together. Something she wasn't sure she was ready for.

"So get an early start. Leave right after breakfast," Charlie shouted with something akin to triumph. He certainly looked smug.

"Look, Charlie—" Sherry began.

"Sherry doesn't have to be at the hospital until this afternoon," said Charlie, cutting her off again, rolling out his idea as if she hadn't uttered a peep. "Sure, it's a longish drive, but from what I hear, it's a beautiful part of the country. You could have lunch in Traverton, and that's near the hospital."

"You want to tell us what to eat while you're at it?" Sherry glared at Charlie sourly. "How about the conversation? Are we allowed to talk about anything we want, or do you want to control that too?"

Charlie's tormented expression was as false as a dozing piranha's. "I don't know, chicken. Here I am, trying to arrange things so you can have a free day in good company, and you accuse me of trying to manipulate you." He sighed. "Just doing my best and getting no thanks, as usual."

"Lunch in Traverton with Sherry sounds fine to me," Carston said, calmly.

But Sherry thought he was looking just as smug as Charlie was.

"You see? He likes the idea too," Charlie exploded triumphantly.

Sherry shook her head. "Carston, be careful. Don't underestimate Charlie-boy here. He starts plotting before he even wakes up in the morning. More than likely, he's told every single journalist in the western world that you and I will be in Traverton today. We won't even be able to play tiddlywinks without being photographed."

****

Under an even gloomier sky, Sherry and Carston contemplated the main street of Traverton. The only sign of bustling activity, aside from a candy wrapper drifting across the road, was an old-timer leaning on a lamppost and scratching his arm.

"The town seems a little on the sleepy side," said Carston.

"I'm glad Charlie said this was the ideal place to have lunch," said Sherry. "As far as I can see, there's one fire hydrant, one grocery store, one hairdresser, a dress shop that features dead flies in its display window, a doubtful-looking bar, one greasy spoon, and not much else."

"There might be a hidden wild side," Carston suggested.

"Even so, it would be a sleepy wild side."

"As far as lunch goes, I guess it's the greasy spoon or die."

"It'll probably be the greasy spoon *and* die. Just when life's looking good." Sherry was grinning.

The diner, ominously called the Paradise Café, was, aside from a dead moth on the floor, empty of clients. A waitress with yellowish hair, leaned against the counter, eyes closed.

"At least you don't have to worry about signing autographs in this place," Carston whispered as he and Sherry slid into a booth. "Unless the moth gets excited."

"Don't have to worry about much of anything," Sherry whispered back. "The waitress is asleep."

"If she were awake, what would you order?"

Sherry shrugged. "A bacon, lettuce, and tomato

49

sandwich without the bacon."

"I'll go for that."

"You don't have to stop eating meat just because I'm a vegetarian."

"Eating meat in front of a vegetarian makes me feel like a savage."

The waitress opened her eyes and, with infinite boredom, slouched over to their table.

Sherry smiled at her. "Why's this place called The Paradise Café?"

The waitress gaped at Sherry for a full minute. Then shrugged. "Beats me."

"Me too. That's why I asked."

"You guys wanna order or what?"

"Two coffees, two bacon, lettuce, and tomato sandwiches without the bacon."

"Suits me fine." The waitress turned slowly and began shuffling in the direction of the counter. Then stopped. Whirled around with sudden and violent energy. Gaped at Sherry. "Hey! You're not Sherry Valentine, are you? You sure look like Sherry Valentine, anyway. I bet you are."

Sherry glanced ruefully at Carston before answering, "I only look like her."

"Nah. Can't fool me. I heard you were going to be down in Midville this week. You *are* Sherry Valentine. And I want your autograph, right?" She raced back, slapped a pen and none-too-clean piece of paper down on the table. "Sherry Valentine. Coming to Traverton. Isn't that something." Her voice was triumphant.

"I haven't exactly come here. I'm only passing through."

"You can have bacon on your sandwich if you

want. Doesn't cost extra."

"No, thank you. No bacon."

The waitress smirked knowingly. "Bet you don't care if it costs. You're so rich it doesn't matter."

"I don't want bacon because I don't eat meat."

The waitress folded the paper with the autograph and tucked it into her pocket. Then looked sly. "Ask you a question?"

Sherry sighed with resignation. "Could I stop you?"

"You still dating Clyde Winter?"

"No." Sherry avoided glancing at Carston across the table. "That's just silly gossip. I never did date Clyde Winter."

"How about Johnny Withlock?"

"No." Sherry looked up beseechingly. There had to be a way to get rid of the woman.

"I read you dropped Johnny Withlock for Clyde Winter, and that Clyde Winter and you are going to get married. I read it in *Star*. And in *Glitzy* too."

"Don't believe what you read in *Star* or *Glitzy*. Never even read *Star* and *Glitzy*. Just line garbage cans with those rags." From under her lashes Sherry finally peeked at Carston. He looked amused.

"I always read them," said the waitress stubbornly. "I love *Star* especially."

"Sherry Valentine doesn't date Johnny Withlock or Clyde Winter because she's with me." Carston's tone was definite.

Sherry stared at him. He only smiled archly at her.

The waitress scrutinized Carston, but he obviously didn't look like any celebrity she'd ever seen in a glossy magazine. "So who are *you*?"

"Carston Hewlett. Playwright."

"Oh." Losing all interest, she turned and disappeared into the kitchen.

"You see," Carston said. His eyes danced. "There are advantages in being on the serious side of art and not in light entertainment. I'll never hit the pages of *Star* or *Glitzy*."

Sherry shook her head ruefully. "Those papers are pure gossip, rumor, and fantasy. They're just awful. And dangerous. They can ruin reputations, destroy relationships. Fortunately, neither *Star* nor *Glitzy* touch on what I really do in music."

"Which is?"

"You really want to know? This could be boring for you."

"Yes, I really want to know. And let me decide what I find boring."

"Fine. Well, a long time ago, I decided I wouldn't be a simple singer of hits because there are thousands of those. What I wanted to do was bring country music back to its roots, to its traditional instrumentation, to its origins in sixteenth- and seventeenth-century European folk songs." She watched him, waited for him to challenge what she was saying.

His voice was mild, not challenging. "Where do you get your information?"

"I've spent years in archives and libraries, reading books on musicology and the history of music. And I've listened to the recordings of old-timers at the Library of Congress. Of course, most people don't realize the amount of work that goes into my compositions." She felt her chin jut out aggressively.

Carston's look was quizzical. "Why are you so

defensive?"

Defensive? He was right. She was feeling defensive. She often did. Not all the time, of course, but now and again...whenever she felt she had to stand up for what she was; or when she thought someone underestimated her and disregarded her work; or when she thought people might sneer because she'd never finished high school. But was Carston doing any of that? Was he being condescending? No. He wasn't.

So she was just over-reacting to that Ivy League image of his, an image that meant good schools, good society, university, and a wealthy caring family—all the things she'd missed out on. Yet she'd made up for the lack, hadn't she? Shown she was worthy of respect, then proved it time and time again.

"I guess I just want to make sure you get the right picture."

"I've been getting the right picture, I'm sure of it." His eyes warm, he reached for her hand and squeezed it gently. "That's why I'm here."

"Oh." Her defiance vanished in a flush of pleasure. Be careful, her inner voice warned again. This is a man with all the right phrases, the ones guaranteed to charm a woman. *A smooth talker, a man of words—isn't that his profession?* She should be watching her every step, not melting like sweet yellow butter in the sun.

The waitress brought their sandwiches and, leaning against the counter, returned to her former torpor. She only opened her eyes when Carston asked for the bill.

"Same price with or without the bacon," she said. "I can't go around changing the rules just because you don't want bacon. A bacon, lettuce, and tomato sandwich is still a bacon, lettuce, and tomato sandwich with or without the bacon."

"Like a glass of water without the glass," said Sherry, idly.

"Or Sherry Valentine without prickles," Carston replied, just as mildly.

Just as they reached the door of the Paradise Café, Sherry half-turned, looked back at the waitress. All her sleepiness had vanished, and cell phone in hand, she was busy punching in a number. Spreading the news that she'd been here with Carston? Well, so what? That waitress probably wouldn't even remember his name.

****

When Carston stopped his car in the parking lot of the children's hospital, Sherry took a tube of lipstick out of her purse.

"You'd look better without that, you know." Then he felt like kicking himself for his rudeness. What right did he have, telling her what to do and how to look? Now she'd be furious.

She wasn't. Instead, she turned to him with a good-natured smile. "Believe me, I hate this slop I smear all over my face, but it's part of the show. The kids in the hospital want to meet the same Sherry they've seen on television. If they don't, they'd think they were getting a fake."

"Actually, that didn't come out the way I intended it to." He felt embarrassed. "I meant something else altogether."

"Oh?" The lipstick tube stayed poised in the air. "And what were you meaning to say?"

"That you have a beautiful mouth. I noticed it the second I met you." He reached out, traced the line of her lips with the tip of his finger. And felt his hand buzz.

"Thanks." Her voice was soft; her eyes flickered. She didn't move to put on the lipstick. Just sat there, staring at him. The softness in her eyes turned him inside out. She had it bad, he decided, and it looked like he was also sitting in the same keel-less boat.

He tried shoving some gruff into his voice. "Come on. Duty calls. The kids are in there, waiting. And about to ask you for your autograph."

"Fine. Can't put them in the same category as blood-thirsty *Star* reporters."

"That's for later. When word gets out we've spent almost the whole day together." The idea gave him a warm spurt of satisfaction. For some crazy reason, he really did like the idea of having his name linked to hers.

"Wait and see how much you'll like that," she warned.

As they left the car, he realized he was feeling strangely nervous. He didn't know any sick children, he didn't know any other children either, and he wasn't a famous singer or entertainer. Right now he was feeling like Sherry Valentine's third wheel. "What am I supposed to do now that I'm here? I don't know what to say to kids. I'm never around any."

"You were an only child?"

"How do you know that?"

Her eyes were mocking. "It's written all over you. I bet your mother thought you were the sun itself, and your father thought you were a genius."

"Of course they did. Still do too. But that doesn't tell me what I should do when we're inside."

Sherry's smile was reassuring. "Stop worrying.

55

You're not expected to do anything. I'm the one they're waiting for. But if you want to participate, it's easy enough. Just talk to the kids. Tell them a story if you feel inspired. They'll probably flood you with questions when they find out you write plays. Sick kids are just like healthy kids anywhere. They just want to have fun, and they deserve a hell of a lot more of it than they're having at the moment."

He wondered how Sherry would handle this, though. Charlie had claimed it wasn't a publicity stunt, but did he really believe that? Surely, this was just another way of being on stage.

But he soon saw how much he'd underestimated the importance of a celebrity appearance. Most of the children had been assembled in a large, bright room; those who couldn't be moved from their beds received a personal visit. And Sherry seemed to know exactly how to talk to each and every one. She did it naturally too, and adoring eyes watched her, took in her every move. One child had even drawn a picture of Sherry.

"A remarkable resemblance," said Carston gravely as he examined the blinding pink blotch. "Picasso couldn't have done it better."

"Please, Miss Valentine, will you sing 'Rocky Mountain Shower'?" asked one diminutive girl, her eyes hopeful.

"If you'll all sing along with me."

So they did. And it sounded fine, all things considered. In fact, there were many things to be considered, Carston decided. Like, how natural Sherry was, how unaffected, and that made her more seductive. Sure, the flashy exterior would always draw ogling men like flowers draw bees. Bees...like himself...humming with pleasure at her company. But her humor, her easy warmth also commanded respect.

Still, that was no reason to forget this was nothing permanent, nothing to take seriously, nothing more than a light, sexual attraction. Why read importance into this encounter? Sherry was a woman of experience— weren't brief, sexual attractions all part of her glittery show business world? Of course they were. Sure *Star* and *Glitzy* printed gossip; sure the waitress in the Paradise Café was only repeating what she'd read about Sherry and those pretty boy stars, Johnny Withlock and Clyde Winter. But even if the information wasn't one hundred percent correct, where there's smoke, there's always fire...

And, come to think of it, since the gossips and the paparazzi would be thinking the worst anyway, why bother driving all the way back to Midville? They could enjoy the rest of the afternoon in each other's company, stop for a romantic dinner, then find a nice hotel somewhere along the road. If she agreed...And judging by her reactions so far, the softness in her eyes when she looked at him, Sherry Valentine wasn't about to object to a night in his arms.

Oh yes. A night of making love was something they'd both enjoy very much, he was sure of it. All he needed to do was remain cool and not too eager, too lusty sounding—if he could manage it. He wasn't so certain he could.

Chapter Five

"Do you have to get back to Midville right away?"

Sherry looked over at Carston, but his expression was neutral, as if her answer didn't matter one way or the other. There was no hint of seduction in his voice, no innuendo.

On the left, just outside the car, the countryside curved into a deep valley where a glancing wind played over ragged grasses; on the right, a forest of blue shadow invited exploration. The sky, still dull, promised rain, but the air was as pungent as fresh chestnuts. She took a deep breath, as if she were already out there, standing under the trees.

"Actually, I don't feel like going back to Midville ever," she answered truthfully. She'd kept her voice as neutral-sounding as he had, but she wanted to draw out this day for as long as possible. Relish the freedom; glory in the absence of crowds. Savor the pleasure of Carston's company.

He smiled at her answer, and his neutrality vanished. He was as pleased as she was. "How about exploring that big thing ahead of us." He gestured to a rocky mountain.

"Sure. Sounds fine. Just as long as we don't have to explore every single inch of it in one afternoon."

"Do you like going for walks?"

"I don't get around to doing much of them. But the

idea sounds great."

Carston turned left, directed the car along the climbing forest road separating them from the gully below. Aside from one farm hidden behind a cluster of trees, there was no sign of human habitation. Several miles further on, the paved surface gave way entirely, became a dirt track.

"End of the line." Carston stopped the car and turned off the engine. "We're lost to the world."

"Don't be so sure," Sherry warned. She pulled out her cell phone, pushed a few keys, and looked amused. "Hey, you know what? You're right. There's no signal up here. Even good old Charlie can't get to us. Isn't that nice? Of course, no phone signal doesn't guarantee anything. Charlie has radar and sonar implants in that heart of his."

They left the car and began wandering over the soft, forest floor. Carston caught her hand, threaded his fingers through hers, and it felt wonderful. Incredible how something so simple could seem intimate and so right. "Isn't this beautiful," she breathed. She knew she wasn't only referring to the landscape.

Carston glanced at her curiously. "Don't you get out into the country very often?"

"Oh yes, I do." She smiled wryly. "I'm constantly leaving one city, roaring through the country, and arriving in the next city."

"How about time off?"

"Oh, I'm allowed to sleep most nights, but it's been so many years since I did anything comparable to this, I'd forgotten what it's like." She looked around her, luxuriated in the resinous air. "Just think, at this very moment, most people in Midville are in offices, or are racing around in cars, or are running into stores and buying things, or are complaining about not being able to own something and feeling depressed about it. And look at this—" Her arm made a wide eloquent gesture that took in the forest, the mountain and the sky. "This is what real luxury is all about."

"Which is why I live in an isolated farmhouse," said Carston.

Surprised, Sherry stopped walking. "You live in an isolated farmhouse? That's the last place I imagined you in."

"Why?"

"I don't know. You're so...so urbane. Therefore urban." She laughed shortly. "I picture you in a very elegant New York apartment, cocktail in hand and surrounded by sophisticated mistresses."

"If that's the image I give off, it's totally misleading," he said. "No elegant New York apartment and rarely a cocktail."

"At least I got one out of three right." She sniffed, tried to hide the sudden ridiculous, totally uncalled-for pinch of jealousy.

He laughed outright, his eyes sparkling mischievously. "Actually, you didn't even get one right. Sophisticated mistresses don't appreciate isolated farmhouses and a man more obsessed by his work than the social whirl. Sophisticated mistresses don't take kindly to long walks over fields or through the woods. For my part, I detest the cocktail parties, clubs, crowds, and impersonal chitchat that sophisticated mistresses seem to favor."

"Looks like we hate the same things then, but Charlie always looks at me as if I'm ready for the glue factory when I say things like that."

They turned onto a sandy path leading between young birch and pine trees, where the tang of mushrooms and damp leaves filled the air.

"How about you?" Carston asked. "What sort of life do you lead?"

"What do you imagine it's like?"

He looked down at her, as if evaluating what he saw. "I don't know, really. I suppose I have the usual stereotype in mind. A country music singer has to live near some wilderness, perhaps on a prairie or in the mountains. But the way you dress, the make-up, the hair, none of that goes along with the great outdoors and a lonely wooden cabin in the back of beyond. And you did just tell me you never get out into the country."

She chuckled. "Actually, I live in a penthouse in Memphis. The closest I get to ranching is herding red spider off my house plants."

"You've been married?"

She nodded. "I have been. Twice."

He waited for her to elaborate. She didn't. "Is this something you'd prefer not talking about?"

She shrugged. "It's not that. It just seems that if you want to learn about someone, there are more important subjects than ex-husbands."

"More important subjects? To my way of thinking, hearing about ex-husbands is definitely a way of learning about someone."

"You can find out all about failed marriages in magazines like *Star* and *Glitzy*. To me, important personal things are favorite books or preferred ice cream flavors."

"You wouldn't happen to be hedging?" But he still

smiled. "And I can promise you, I'll never read *Star*."

She shrugged. "Okay. It's just…Well, I suppose there's not an awful lot to say about either marriage, not the first, and not the second. Neither one was programmed to last. They were just a mixture of show business confusion and crossed wires. I suppose they were inevitable, in some way."

"How were they inevitable?"

"Wanting a home was essential to me back then. So was security. You see, my own mother got pregnant, but she didn't want a child. I never knew who my father was. I certainly wasn't a happy kid because I just didn't believe anyone could ever love me. So I just rebelled against everything. The one really good thing I did do, was start singing in a choir when I was twelve. I loved it."

"Don't quite a few singers get started that way?"

"They do. Being in a choir is great training, and it gives you the feeling of belonging somewhere. But because I was rebellious, I ran away from home on my sixteenth birthday. My idea was to hit Nashville and get discovered, but that didn't happen instantly. There are millions of people trying to break into the music world."

"And very few actually make it."

"Absolutely true. But pure belief and determination can carry you a long way. For years, I struggled along, worked at every job you can think of, as a waitress, a barmaid, a dog walker, a dog groomer, anything, and I sang wherever I could—in bars, parties, at backwoods music festivals. And the whole time, I haunted libraries and read about traditional music. Then, one day, I met Bobby Blake, and he became my first husband."

"Even I've heard his name, and I know nothing about the country music scene." The warmth in Carston's voice had vanished. "And being Bobby Blake's wife got you where you wanted to be."

She stopped walking, peered up at him. Saw the nerve ticking in his jaw. What was going on? Why was he sounding so suspicious, so… bitter? "That's unfair," she countered. "This is my story and you have to let me tell it my way."

"Sorry." He relaxed slightly.

She'd obviously hit a nerve, though. His eyes were wary, and his posture was defensive. "I bet I know what you're thinking," she said slowly.

"Really?"

"Really." She wasn't put off by the chill in his voice. "You've decided I was an ambitious young nobody who slept with and snagged a star in the music world. That I used him to promote my act and divorced him when I was well known."

From his expression, she was certain she'd hit the nail on the head, but he merely shrugged. "Let's just say that's the sort of situation I'm quite familiar with. I can't begin to tell you how many actors and actresses have found me very attractive ever since I made a name for myself. And those are usually the ones who pretended I didn't exist during the long years when I was a struggling writer."

"Well, if you think I'm like that, you're wrong," she said heatedly. "I never used Bobby Blake. This was many years ago, way back when. And way back then, Bobby Blake was just starting out, like me. All we did was join forces to fight our way into the music business as a winning combination. On stage, at least."

"And offstage? Didn't love come into the picture?"

"I'm not sure it did. For me, Bobby was a friend and a partner, although he was a very possessive one. He was the one who pushed for marriage, and that marriage was no fun at all. Bobby became violently jealous. He spied on me, had detectives prying into my every move. Things got so bad, I couldn't even go to a supermarket without him following me, screaming at me, threatening me, accusing me of flirting with every man on the street. In the end, I wasn't even allowed to talk to our musicians. I had no choice but to leave if I wanted to be a singer—or if I wanted to survive."

"And the second marriage?"

"Another disaster. Our manager, Terry Linden, hid me from Bobby who was trying to force me to come back and threatening to kill me if I didn't. I was so grateful to Terry for his protection. He kept me feeling safe, but security isn't the same thing as love. After hanging on in there for too many years, we finally admitted we had nothing in common and that our marriage was a mistake."

"No children?"

"I never thought it would be right to impose an itinerant life style on children. As old-fashioned as it sounds, I really do believe the word family means a mother, a father, and a stable home life. And I've never thought nannies and *au pairs* are a good solution either. What about you?"

"Me?" He shook his head. "Hard to imagine myself with children. I was married once, a long time ago and very briefly, but I've never had the desire to marry again or even live with anyone."

"Never?"

"Never. I'm a writer, and I need solitude. I love it. I'm a dyed-in-the-wool loner. I hate telephones, fax machines, and I avoid the Internet as much as I can. I don't even own a cell phone. You see? Anti-social. Therefore, I'm not the right person for a lasting relationship and the social demands that would entail."

"The way my attempts at marriage went, I suppose I could say the same thing," Sherry said slowly. But his words piqued her. Well, at least she could give him credit for being honest about what the rules of the game were: no promises, no future. Whatever happened over the next few days—if they became lovers, if feelings deepened—this would still never be more than a fling.

They walked in silence for a while. Until Carston released her fingers, curled his arm around her shoulders. Sherry caught her breath, then nestled her head into his shoulder; it felt right, there, as if that were the perfect place for it. His warm scent floated up to her nostrils, wonderful, intoxicating, and dangerous.

He looked down at her, and she saw his desire met her own. Lowering his head, he took her mouth softly, his tongue feathering her lips. She half turned, pressed herself against the hardness of his muscular male body, curled her arms around his neck, then felt the world spin away. A kiss? This was a voyage into another dimension. The kiss turned into another, then another, until her blood sizzled, and her body cried out for more.

The need for air forced them apart, and they clung to each other.

"Powerful stuff," he murmured into her hair.

She could only nod. Words had vanished. The intensity she felt with this man had dragged her far away from the everyday world and normal conversation.

He pulled back slightly, and his eyes, warm, gleaming, met hers. "It's lovely being with you, Sherry Valentine." His voice was low, intense.

She managed to nod dreamily. "Ditto," she whispered. Lovely being beside him, talking with him, seeing his smile, hearing his ideas. Equally lovely, the thought of making love with him. How she wanted him. She wanted his naked skin under her fingertips, her body stretched out beside his. She wanted this man who was still almost a stranger. But wasn't that the way things went in flings? The thought chilled her, cut into the good feeling. Involuntarily she took half a step back.

"Is something the matter?" His eyes were concerned.

"Just wondering," she said. "Wondering about where this is leading. A few hot nights together before the festival ends. Then *adios*. Nice to have met you."

"Is there something wrong with two people finding out they want each other? Or enjoying each other in bed, and out of it?"

"No. Nothing." Or nothing she could talk about so casually. How could she say she already knew she'd miss him when they parted? That she wanted to learn more about him, spend more time with him, talking, doing simple things—things like walking through forests. Or visiting nowhere places like Traverton. Could she say she didn't want this to be a casual encounter? That he'd already touched her heart in some indefinable way? That she cared for him? And that caring for someone who only wanted a passing fling was painful?

No. She couldn't say that. If she did, he'd think she was a very clingy sort of person, someone who glued herself to any man, someone impossible to get rid of, and he'd go racing over that mountain, desperate to get away.

"I was also thinking of the repercussions of this…thing…between the two of us," she said calmly.

"Thing?" His face was unreadable, but she was certain he was still on fling-waveband.

"Yes. *Thing.* One-night stands or three-day flings at conferences and festivals. It's not the sort of *thing* I do. And thanks to the press, absolutely everybody in the whole country will know about it. And that turns this into…" She stopped. Searching for words? Or excuses? Or a way of avoiding pain?

He watched her closely for a few seconds. "All right," he said slowly. "Forgive me for misjudging the situation." His fingers traced the line of her cheekbone, and his expression was tender. "It's your fault, you know. You're just so damned sexy." He kissed her once more, very briefly this time. Then curled her fingers into his again. "How about if we discuss the complications over candlelight, a good dinner, and a bottle of wine. Especially since it's going to rain any minute now."

Gratefully, Sherry let out her breath. He wouldn't pressure her. She could trust him. Then she looked up at the sky. Thick clouds had moved in and a sudden violent wind was tossing the treetops. "I didn't notice how dark the sky's become. Looks like we're in for a storm."

"We certainly are."

The sky turned a deeper shade of black, but they

managed to reach the car before the rain fell. When it did, the countryside around them vanished. Hurled by the wind, strong trees bent like gelatin, and gushing torrents flattened grasses, dragged branches, pine needles and mud along the road.

Carston turned his key in the ignition, started the motor, turned up the heat, and slowly inched down the slippery mountain road. It was rough going; only when they reached the paved surface did steering become less difficult. Still, it was hard to ignore the looming mountain hemming them in on the left, the sheer drop into the valley on the right. Without the protection of the forest, the little car shuddered violently in the wind.

Seemingly unperturbed, Carston drove on steadily. Out of the corner of her eye, Sherry watched his strong hands on the steering wheel, his calm face. He was wonderful-looking; his sharply delineated features, the deep laugh lines, all underlined a strong, determined character. And his male aura? That was so definite it was almost tangible; it filled the tiny space, had every nerve in her body responding—despite the dreary little inner voice telling her, again and again, he was definitely not a man she could count on.

A sudden jerk and the squeal of brakes shot her out of her reverie. The car skidded on the slippery surface of the road, and then stalled. Ahead of them in the dim light she could just make out a dark mass.

"What is it?"

He looked puzzled. "I'm not sure."

Fighting the buffeting wind, they climbed out of the car, made their way over to the obstacle. A huge tree lay directly across the road. "The storm must have brought that down," Carston shouted over the wind.

"Lucky we weren't driving through when it did."

Sherry nodded, held back the curls whipping violently across her face. They certainly had been lucky. Sort of. Because there was no way they could move that tree, and there was no way to drive around it.

They fought their way back to the relative calm of the car's interior.

"Now what?

Carston peered down the deserted road. "No use waiting for rescue. No one will come up here in a storm like this, especially since the road comes to a dead end. Besides, no one knows we're up here." He was still perfectly calm, she noted. He wasn't seething with fury or anguish, as most people would be when confronted by nature's vagaries. He was just the sort of man you needed in an emergency.

"You don't seem worried that we're miles from civilization—if anyone can apply the word civilization to Traverton. And the weather probably won't get better soon."

He looked at her with smiling amusement. "How far would worrying get me? Of course, if I'd planned this out in advance, I'd have arranged for the tree to come down in front of a very romantic hotel with no telephones, but a comfortable room containing a nice big bed. As it is, we can't spend the night in this car. It's not even big enough to pull your socks off in." His smile widened. "And, by the way, you don't look very worried either."

"Why should I be? The tree missed us. We're safe and sound." If he wasn't angry or upset or worried, why should she be? Wasn't this just another shared adventure? One she would tuck away in that corner of her brain reserved for cherished memories.

"We could telephone for help," he said. "If there's a signal here."

"Of course we can. I forgot all about my cell phone." Telephones seemed ridiculously prosaic in a situation like this. She pulled out her phone. Looked. "Nope. Still no signal. So now what?"

"We passed a farm on the way up. I don't know how far away it is. I'll walk down, see if the farmer has a tractor to shift the tree. Or, at worst, a saw or an axe. You wait here, in the car." He pointed to the keys. "If you get cold, just run the engine."

"Why do I have to wait in the car?" Sherry asked, ignoring the keys. "I'm no delicate flower. I can walk just as well and as far as you can."

"He-man stuff," he said, his voice almost gruff. "Protective male instinct. You know the sort of thing I mean. It isn't raining much now, but it might start again soon. If you stay in the car, you'll be dry."

"And bored."

"I'm only trying to make life easy for you. In that beaded blouse and fringed jacket, those tight jeans and fancy boots, you look like you belong on a stage under bright spotlights, not on a deserted road in a storm." He raised his hand in warning. "And don't get me wrong. I'm not saying the outfit doesn't look good. It does. It's sexy as hell. Just not road-worthy."

"Oh come on." She was scornful. "I grew up in Dog's Pass. You're the one who should be worried. You probably spent your whole childhood in some prissy private school."

He ignored her comment. "There could be more than five or six miles to walk before we get to that farmhouse."

"So what are we waiting for? Look at the sky."

Carston shrugged. "Please yourself."

Sherry reached for the door handle, then stopped. "Did you really go to a prissy school?"

"Of course I did. Where else? I majored in needlework at Yale too." He looked down at her boots. "You really think you can cover a few miles in those? Aren't cowboy boots meant for riding on horses?"

"Gosh, they sure do teach you an awful lot in those needlework classes."

They set out, pushed by the wind. Five or six miles *was* far, Sherry said to herself. Even two miles was far, but she'd rather find work as a galley slave than admit that to Carston. Maybe he'd over-estimated the distance? She hoped so. These boots of hers were most definitely not made for walking: her left heel was hinting that it no longer wanted to be part of her life. But if she curled up her toes and put her weight on the outer edge of her foot, she'd certainly survive the torture of a rubbing boot.

They walked at a brisk pace. More of Carston's he-man stuff? She didn't think so. She couldn't help noticing how often he looked up at the sky. He wanted to get to that farm fast; in that elegant tweed jacket, silk shirt, and fine shoes, he wasn't more suitably dressed for bad weather than she. Besides, she wanted to show him she could handle any challenge nature threw at her…just so long as he didn't get suspicious, ask her too many questions about Dog's Pass, about the backwoods upbringing she'd always bragged about.

The sky above flared white with a sudden blaze of lightning.

"You all right?" Carston asked. Reaching for Sherry's hand, he pulled her alongside him. "You're probably not even afraid, are you?"

"Am I supposed to be?"

"You have a knack for making me feel silly," he growled. "Of course you're not supposed to be afraid. Just most people are. And if you're not frightened, I still can't use my he-man act."

"Perhaps just being human is enough?"

"The thought did cross my mind. Where you're concerned." His eyes were warm, oh so warm.

"Good." She grinned back. "You know what? I'm having fun." She was. She hadn't enjoyed herself this much in a long time. Carston's long fingers were curled together with hers; his determined profile was wonderfully framed against the evening's ominous light. And each time their eyes met, she saw a tenderness that had nothing to do with the fleeting sentiments of a light-hearted affair. Not that he'd admit such a thing to her—or even to himself.

"Tell me, what does scare you?" he asked.

"Starving crocodiles. I can pretty well talk my way out of any awful situation, but where do you begin with crocodiles?"

No cars passed, but the rain held off until dusk. As the first drops slapped the ground, Sherry could just make out a thicket of trees beyond the next turning. "I think that's where the farm is."

"You're right. Let's get there before the weather gets worse." They jogged across a wooden bridge above a churning river. Straight ahead was the house, its outline blurred by dark and rain. Heads down, they raced toward the front porch and bounded up the steps.

Stopped.

The house was a ruin. Its windows gaped blindly, the door hung crazily ajar, and the roof had long ago cascaded into the dark interior. The place had been abandoned for years.

This time Carston insisted she wait in the shelter of the sagging porch while he went in search of somewhere more comfortable. "Maybe there's another building, a barn or a shack, someplace where we can keep out of the rain." He followed a track through the long grass and found a large barn, its large door wide open. Aside from a few leaks, it seemed relatively dry; at least the roof was still in place. Then he went back to fetch Sherry.

"Our luck is still holding. Wait till you see this." He slung his arm over her shoulders and, holding her close to his warmth, led the way.

"Hay," Sherry said as soon as they were inside the barn. "I can smell hay."

"Straw, not hay," he corrected, but the mistake woke up his curiosity...again. "You'd think a country girl would know the difference."

She turned to stare at him defiantly. "And since when is Mr. Ivy League an expert on animal fodder?"

"Ever since I fell passionately in love with Stagger."

"Stagger?"

He grinned. "My beautiful gray mare. I was eight years old when she came into my life."

"Oh."

"So I can assure you that hay is the very nutritious mix of grasses that animals eat, and straw is dried cereal stalks. You use it for bedding animals down or, in my grandparent's time, filling mattresses. There's a pile of it over there, near the back wall. We can build a nest and keep warm if we're stuck here for the night."

Her eyes glittered. "A night spent in the straw?"

Didn't sound at all bad, spending the night here with Sherry in his arms. It wasn't a luxury hotel, but that didn't seem to matter to her, strangely enough. In fact, he was feeling extraordinarily grateful to her. How many other women of his acquaintance would have accepted this situation? None. Sherry hadn't ranted about the tree lying across the road; she hadn't complained about the distance they'd walked. And she wasn't fussing about wind-blown hair, running mascara, or being stranded.

Of course, he still had to offer to do the gentlemanly thing: "If you don't mind staying here alone and waiting, I could try and reach Traverton. Find a car or a taxi, and come pick you up."

"I don't mind being here alone. But why would you want to walk all that way through the night in the pouring rain? It'll take you hours to get to Traverton. Let's just wait. The storm might be over in the morning, but even if it isn't, there might be some traffic on the road."

Oh yes, she was gutsy, all right. And he liked that. A lot. His respect for her grew even more although he wasn't feeling so sure about the implications. When you liked and respected someone, how did you smile, wave, say, "Good-bye, it's been fun"? This brief affair just might be more complicated than he'd thought. Or was willing to think.

They stood in the barn's open door, watched the rain lashing the ground, listened to the roar of the nearby river. He felt her shiver and pulled her more tightly into the fold of his arms. He loved the way she covered his hands with her own, the way she curled against him. He loved breathing in the warm scent of her skin—a natural scent, far headier than any man-made perfume could ever be. It wouldn't be bad if time stopped now, if this moment went on for eternity.

She turned her head slightly, looked up at him with warm eyes, a lazy smile floating over her lips. His fingers sought her face, pushed back the damp curls from her forehead and cheeks. This whole situation was too romantic. Too dramatic and too intense. He tried to lighten the atmosphere. "You don't mind being stuck here all night?"

"What's the choice? You ever slept in straw before?"

"Of course I have."

"Come on. Carston Hewlett, famous playwright, sleeping in straw?"

"Okay, country girl, when was the last time you slept in straw?"

"It'll kill me to admit this." She laughed. "Never."

"Then I'd better warn you: straw is highly overrated. It's scratchy and nothing like a warm blanket."

"I'll probably survive that." She snuggled closer to him.

She was driving him crazy. With each passing second, he melted a little more. And wondered what the hell was going on. This was lust? Again, he pushed down the strange emotions. "How about all the man-eating spiders living in straw?"

"Man-eating spiders? As long as they've got you,

I'm fine," Sherry said smugly. "I've always known that being female has some great advantages."

"Aren't you afraid of spiders either?"

She smirked. "I'm supposed to be afraid of something that's smaller than my fingernail?"

Nice fingernails, he thought with satisfaction. Not painted, not long. Just oval-shaped and pretty.

The rain let up temporarily, but another bright flash of lightning streaked through the sky, was followed by a harsh clap of thunder and wild gust of wind. He felt Sherry tense against the chill. Cowboy spangles obviously weren't much good as insulating material. He would make her as warm, as comfortable as possible. Even if the raw materials weren't up to much. "Okay, shall we test tonight's bed?"

"First, I'm going back out to that river we passed to wash up. I don't mind sharing a straw bed with spiders, or many-footed insects, or mice, rats, raccoons, or even skunks. But what I would hate is spending the whole night with this goopy makeup on my face."

Carston smiled to himself. He didn't know many women who'd react like that either. He began inspecting the far reaches of the barn and scraped together enough clean straw to make a luxurious pile in the driest corner. By the time Sherry returned, their makeshift bed was ready.

"What will we do in the morning?" she asked as she pulled off her boots.

"I'll walk as far as I can and find help. Or at least I'll walk until I pick up a signal on your phone. You can wait here."

"There you go again. Just imagine if I'd stayed in the car this afternoon, waiting for you. By now I'd be thinking you'd been snacked on by bears. And you'd have had to walk through the rain all the way back to the car just to tell me this place was deserted." She snuggled into their improvised bed. Carston covered her with a thick layer of straw and folded his arms around her once again.

"Beats a wet road any day," she murmured.

"You're really okay?"

"Perfectly."

She'd say that anyway, he knew. Whether or not she was comfortable. That's the sort of person she was: positive when all the odds were against her. He was grateful, and felt the urge to offer her even more. Funny how the human character worked: the less she demanded, the more he felt like giving. And her head with its damp curls felt just right nestled into the crook of his arm.

"Warm enough?"

"Now I am."

"Definitely not the way I planned out the evening."

"Just how did you plan it?" her voice teased.

"With you in my arms. After that candle-lit dinner and bottle of wine."

"The dinner and candlelight are flops. But I'm in the right place."

"You are." His voice was husky. Yes, she was in the right place, all right. But they weren't on a bed. With no clothes on. Making passionate love. Or not yet.

He took off his jacket, tucked it around them, then let his fingers trace her cheek, trail down to the long line of her neck. Her skin was cold. Still not complaining, though. And he remembered how, only a few hours ago, when they'd been walking in the woods, he'd more or less accused her of using Bobby Blake to get where she'd wanted in the world of music. What a fool he was. What a cad. As if someone as natural, as open as Sherry, would do something like that. He owed her an apology. And an explanation.

Because Sherry Valentine wasn't anything like Cynthia, his ex. Cynthia, whose ambition and unfaithfulness had destroyed their marriage. Sherry wasn't even an actress. She was a singer. What possible career benefit could she get from a connection with him? None. She just enjoyed being with him in the same way he enjoyed being with her. And they wanted each other.

What did it matter if this was no luxury hotel room, that there were no silky sheets? The tangy scent of damp earth outside the barn blended into the sweet smell of dry straw. Was she still reluctant to embark on a brief affair? Hadn't the day's events created a bond?

Then he stopped thinking. Bending his head, he caressed her lips with his, and her involuntary sigh of pleasure was all the encouragement he needed. Under the first gentle brush of his tongue, her lips parted and he plundered her mouth, pulled her against his hardness. He wanted her to feel what she did to him, how much he wanted her. Her fingers clutched his shirt, held tight as she arched her hips into his. His hands slid upwards to the fullness of her breasts, and her nipples budded under the caress of his thumbs.

"This has to come off,' he murmured. Slowly he began undoing the pearly snaps of her shirt.

"It does," she sighed. "And this too." Her fingers tugged at his buttons.

Suddenly, she stopped moving. He felt her stiffen,

then pull back. Propping herself up on one elbow, she stared in the direction of the open barn door. "Didn't you hear that?"

"Hear what?" What was going on? Why was she stopping when everything felt so good? Fighting down frustration and annoyance, he came sliding back into the real world. And heard...What? A flock of strange wild birds? Animals? No...human screams that untangled themselves, became intelligible words.

"Come on. Straight ahead."

And a soaked and very shrill troop of boy scouts came pounding in through the barn's open door.

Chapter Six

Sherry opened her eyes. Blinked. Where was she? Half-buried in a pile of prickly straw. The evening's events returned. The storm. The barn. Carston's kisses. Desire. Then the noisy arrival of boy scouts and their troop leader. And what had promised to be a sensual evening had become something else altogether: a friendly evening spent around a campfire—which had been nice enough in quite another way. And when it was finally time to go to sleep, she'd curled into Carston's arms again, as if that was exactly where she belonged.

How nice that had been. So very nice. Where was Carston now?

She raised herself onto one elbow. The lumpy sleeping bags of the scouts spread out across the barn floor resembled a cluster of beached whales. And beyond the barn door, in a blaze of golden sunshine, sat Carston, chatting with the troop leader beside another crackling fire.

She watched him, admired the tousle of his hair, his warm smile. He'd said he was a loner? How could he be? He was so charming, sociable. And tender. To her knowledge, that wasn't how loners behaved. What if he was just trying to protect himself? From what? Feeling? Loving?

He must have felt her watching him. He looked up,

their eyes locked, and her heart turned over. With tenderness…and something else. Something soft, delicate. Something very much like love.

Love? Impossible. Sherry Valentine didn't fall in love—not at this point in her life anyway. She'd had her share of passionate attractions of course. Wasn't that what this was? Well, call it what she liked, she had the feeling everything would be different now. She'd never forget Carston, never forget how good it felt being with him, laughing with him, rambling through a forest with him, sharing the same rather ironic humor…and desire.

If that isn't the beginning of love, what is it?

Would this brief relationship make her happy? Perhaps it wouldn't. But a brief affair with Carston Hewlett would be all she could have. He'd warned her, made it clear. No attachments. And she didn't have time for attachments either. She had a career, a whole life. It had taken her years to build her independence, and she enjoyed every single moment of it. She didn't need to plan for a future, and she was old enough, resourceful enough, to relish her own company.

Caught in the haze of emotion, she watched him turn, pick up a tin cup, dip it into a pot on the fire. Then, with that slow and easy grace that was his alone, he rose to his feet, strode over to where she sat and held out the cup. "Coffee. No sugar, no milk." He grimaced. "Not much taste either."

"Who cares? As long as it's hot." Gratefully she reached out, took the cup, and smiled brightly to hide her heart's wild fluttering.

He sat down beside her, picked out pieces of straw from her hair. "You slept soundly."

"Didn't you?"

He smiled. "As soundly as you did, much to my surprise."

"Surprise?"

Carston's voice dropped. "I had my doubts last night. I thought that holding you in my arms would be more likely to keep me awake than put me to sleep. Despite the presence of fifteen scouts."

"I guess that means I'm less desirable than you imagined," she fished.

"Oh no." His eyes blazed. "Not less."

"Good news." Her voice sounded husky to her own ears.

"That's not the only good news. You see that blue sky and that sun?"

"I do." She sipped the brew. Made a face. "Lovely hot dishwater, this."

He smiled. "There are miles to walk before we find anything better. You feel up to that?"

"Of course I do. Just so long as there's something resembling breakfast at the far end." Or even a place where her cell phone could pick up a signal. Charlie Bacon was probably spitting bullets over their prolonged and unexplained absence. She hoped he hadn't done something drastic like call the police.

"By the way, I tested that river of yours this morning." He grinned ruefully. "It's icy cold. I barely survived."

She grinned back. "Of course it is. It was icy last night too, and I'm going to risk it again. For me, water is water, cold or hot. Back in the days when I was really poor, I saved all the money I could and bought a car. It was a battered old wreck, but I needed something that would get me to singing engagements. Some of the places I went to were so far off the beaten track, you needed bloodhounds to find them. Of course, paying for hotel rooms was out of the question, so I slept in the car. I was always on the look-out for a good river or stream to wash in." She stopped, waited for his reaction—either shock, or disgust. Certainly his own well-off background wouldn't have prepared him for the downside of poverty. Would it affect the way he saw her?

But he wasn't shocked. "A tough lady." His tone was admiring. He trailed his fingers along her jaw.

"Tough? Me?"

"You."

"I wonder." She shrugged. She'd never seen herself that way. As a rebel, yes. As a determined woman. But deep inside, she was far less confident than her public persona let on.

She finished the mug of horrible coffee. Now, where were those spangled boots of hers? She glared sourly at them: it was going to be torture walking anywhere. She sighed inwardly, then reached for them, pulled them on. Stood and took a few steps. Painful, yes, but she'd get used to it. She headed for the river: icy water was going to feel wonderful against her skin.

After washing, fluffing her curls into a semblance of order, she stood and took in her surroundings. Bird song filled the morning air, and from the deep valley below, a pale mist was rising slowly. It was a wonderful place, the country—she'd never appreciated it so much before. In fact, the whole world seemed to be a very wonderful place. And right now, the man who was making her heart sing waited for her beyond that dirt track. So what if they had only two or three days together? She'd live them to the full.

After saying goodbye to the scouts, they set out for Traverton, their heels tapping lightly on the road's surface.

"It's beautiful here," she said softly.

He smiled down at her. "It certainly is. Early morning's always the best part of the day."

"You're an early morning person?"

"I am."

"Me too." Another thing they had in common.

Carston stopped. "Listen."

A noise, high and hysterical, intruded on the morning's peace.

"What is it?"

"Chain saws." He looked pleased.

"Lumberjacks?"

He nodded. "I imagine so."

"Glory be!" Sherry exclaimed. "Breakfast is creeping into the picture after all. Fried eggs, home fries, toast with melting butter, and milky coffee, here I come."

****

Over the phone, Charlie's chuckle sounded like the ominous rumble of a *Tyrannosaurus rex*. "That's what I like about you, chicken. When you go for something, you go for it in a big way. You always know where you're headed."

Sherry felt her anger rise, but a quick glance across the table told her that this wasn't the moment to show it. Once again, she was in the Paradise Café in Traverton, and Carston was right across the table from her, sipping his third cup of coffee. He couldn't even pretend not to hear. As for the sleepy waitress, she was perfectly wide awake, breathing down Sherry's neck, eavesdropping, hanging on every word. She'd probably never heard of such concepts as discretion or privacy, Sherry thought sourly. Coping with Charlie in private was always bad enough. Who needed an audience?

"You sure you don't want to tape this?" Sherry muttered.

The waitress didn't bat an eyelid. Sarcasm wasn't part of her world either.

"Listen to me, Charlie," Sherry said. "You've got it all wrong. There was this tree lying across the road. We got some lumberjacks to drive us back to the car. Then it took time for them to saw the tree up. At the moment, we're in a restaurant in Traverton, having brunch."

"Just think. Three days ago, you walk into the radio station and Mister Playwright-big-shot-Ivy-League looks at you like you have antlers. One day later, he's making goo-goo eyes at a cocktail party. And then, what happens? You both disappear into a love nest."

Nest? He wasn't that far off. Bits of straw had worked their way down under her shirt and wedged themselves between her lacy bra and skin. She was itching like a dog with fleas.

"Charlie! That's the whole story, right? Nothing omitted."

"It's a good story, chicken. We've all heard ones just like it plenty of times. Tree lying across the road? Your phone not picking up signals? Oh sure. How about running out of gas? Or getting a flat tire and having no spare? Or lost car keys? Or a dead battery?" His snort of ridicule came through, loud and clear.

"Now you listen to me—"

"I know. Here it comes again."

"What comes again?" Her teeth were so tightly clenched, she could hardly move her lips.

"The bit about Dog's Pass and the boy next door? Well, that goody-goody next door won't like this story one bit."

"There isn't any story." She rolled her eyes heavenwards. Half an inch away, the waitress sniffed with disbelief. Sherry turned to her. "Go away. Please, just go away." She indicated Carston with a jut of her chin. "Go serve him another cup of coffee."

"He already had two free refills. You gotta pay for another cup, you want more." Her voice was a plaintive whine.

Impossible to miss Carston's snigger. At least he was enjoying this.

Sherry's glared at the waitress. "I'm making this personal. Go away. Please go away. This is a private conversation."

"Lost me, chicken," said Charlie. "What's personal? And what do I mean by what?"

"What you said about the boy next door."

"Come on, kid. You're a big name. Mister Ivy League's big time too. Last anybody saw, the two of you were sashaying out the hotel's front door and gazing at each other like love-stuck teenagers. And that was yesterday morning."

"This is incredible. Really incredible. Teenagers. I can't even talk to a man without everybody deciding we're headed for the closest patch of dark shrubbery."

"Then you don't show up last night," continued Charlie, as imperturbable as usual. "I was worried. You don't show up, your phone doesn't ring. You could've had an accident."

"Don't pretend, you old fake. Everyone knows you have no human emotion. You only worry about losing money."

"I know you think I have a cash register instead of heart, but it's not true. I'm your agent, your manager, and your personal slave driver, but I'm also the best friend you've got. I love you like a daughter." There was a hurt, sentimental note in his voice.

"Okay, okay. Don't go all mawkish on me." But she was touched anyway. "Save the smooth talk for May."

"May doesn't even like me," Charlie lamented. May was his long-suffering wife. They'd been together for over thirty years, although Charlie had been on the road for most of that time. May threatened to leave him several times a year, and usually packed all her bags before changing her mind. "Then because there's no report of an accident near Traverton, I figured the two of you wanted to be alone. So I told myself to stop worrying."

Sherry gave a sigh of relief. "So no scandal, right?"

"Wrong."

"Wrong?" She straightened up again, tense as a rattler.

"It's all Lila Patterson's fault."

Sherry made a face at her telephone. "Oh really? And who might she be?"

"Mister Playwright's leading lady. Gorgeous, too. Black hair, violet eyes, tall, slender. You know: a face that would launch a thousand ships."

The sharp serrated knife of pure jealousy sliced through Sherry's heart. "Times have changed, Charlie.

What modern woman wants to look like diesel fuel?"

"She says Mister Playwright was supposed to meet her plane last night. She was hopping mad by the time she got to the hotel. When he didn't show up for their dinner date, she threw a full scale drama, actress style."

"Interesting." Very interesting indeed. Sherry threw Carston a suspicious look. He hadn't said anything about a leading lady—one who had the right to throw temper tantrums if he wasn't on call. Hadn't he'd declared himself as free as a bird? Yes, he had— and she remembered every single word of all their conversations...or she *thought* she did. Maybe she'd been so busy staggering around on cloud nine that she'd missed out on a few important details? Or perhaps he hadn't been entirely truthful? Because that's the way the landscape was rolling out at this very moment...

"Then there's the journalist from *Star*."

"Oh no. Don't tell me this. Oozing out from under the rocks."

"Seems someone called that rag, told them Sherry Valentine had a new man. And that Sherry Valentine had announced she was dropping the big boys like Johnny Withlock and Clyde Winter. Did that really happen? Did you really say that?"

Sherry only groaned.

"Things are getting interesting," said Charlie with great satisfaction. "I like it."

Furiously Sherry clicked off her phone.

"Bad news?" Carston raised a wonderful eyebrow. He didn't look concerned, not really. And why the hell did he have to look so good? Traitor. That lean jaw, those gray eyes, the bristles of a one-day beard, the errant curl on his forehead. Violet-eyed brunettes probably looked great standing beside him.

"Looks like hell for you." Sherry forced herself to smile archly, then drank down the rest of her cold coffee with what she hoped was a reasonable semblance of detachment.

"I see," said Carston. He still only looked amused. He waited but Sherry said nothing more, merely looked around the room in a bored way. "And who looks like diesel fuel?" he prompted.

She threw him what she hoped was a very dirty look. "Why don't you and this waitress get together and compare notes?"

He wasn't even slightly embarrassed. "You and Charlie were so busy shouting, neither one of you really needed a telephone."

"Well, here's the news: Lila Patterson is on the warpath. You were supposed to pick her up and take her to dinner." She waited for his reaction: shock, distress, misery, or embarrassment.

"Oh. Is that all?" He shrugged. "So what? Obviously she made it from the airport to the hotel. She didn't get lost, wasn't forced to sleep in a barn, or wash in a freezing cold river. I bet she even gets free coffee refills."

No. She had to admit he didn't look like a worried man. Far from it. Her suspicions began to ebb. But what if he was just a good actor? An actor who did an excellent job of hiding uncomfortable feelings such as worry? Or guilt?

"But I suppose we really should head back to Midville and the festival." There wasn't much enthusiasm in his voice.

Sherry sighed. "If we can. If we haven't fallen into

some sort of time warp, or some alternative Bermuda Triangle. You know what I mean: once in Traverton, always in Traverton."

"It's a possibility, I suppose. But we still have to make an effort before taking out a mortgage." He stopped suddenly and looked puzzled. As if a strange thought had just crossed his mind…or as if he wasn't quite sure what he wanted to say. "Sherry?"

"Yes?"

He hesitated. Shook his head slowly before meeting her gaze. "I've enjoyed myself. Very much."

Her breathing stopped. "Ditto." It was the only word she could manage without giving everything away. Without coming out with wild, uncalled-for, and unwanted declarations.

"We're sticking to our plan, aren't we?"

"A deal's a deal." She noticed how her voice trembled and hoped he hadn't heard it too.

"And the candlelit dinner, that's still on, too?"

"I'm looking forward to it." Her heart soared, weightless.

****

"So the lovebirds make it back to civilization." Charlie Bacon was sitting in the armchair in her hotel room, gumming his stinky cigar. He was an immovable force.

"You super-glued into that chair, Charlie-boy? Because, if not, you're out of here. I want a shower, a nap, some free time to myself."

"Cute, both of you vanishing like that." It was as if she hadn't even opened her mouth.

Since there was obviously no way to get rid of him fast, she could try ignoring him. Charlie loathed being ignored. Sherry turned toward the dressing table mirror, began showing a sudden intense interest in her hairstyle, brushing her curls forward, tying them in a knot, shaking them out again. She wasn't interested in a cozy little gossip. She only wanted to be alone. Collect her thoughts. Remember. Run all the good memories through her mind, get them into some semblance of order. Try and control the crazy, dangerous feelings of want and excitement. Just so she didn't make an utter fool of herself as soon as she got near Carston again. And here was Charlie, a solid heap in her room, eating away into precious private think-time and about to ask her questions to which she had no answers. Or even if she had answers, she wasn't about to share them. Because what would Charlie do with them? Dream up a scheme, plan away her life.

"Those journalists down in the lobby, they get their hands on you yet?"

"Nope. No one saw us, aside from cooks, waitresses, and a few grilling chickens. We snuck in through the kitchen." She looked at Charlie triumphantly. "Carston's brilliant idea. After he saw all the cars in the parking lot." She looked at Charlie, her eyes narrowing suspiciously. "And I bet you were the one who set up that mob down in the lobby."

"I didn't set up a thing. I didn't have to. The two of you managed it all on your own."

"Oh sure. Have I ever told you how much I love having no personal life? Being a product?"

"Not so many years ago, you spent nights tossing and turning, wishing the press would notice you more, wishing you'd have real fans—even one or two of them. So I don't take the complaints seriously. I know better."

"Okay, that was back then. These days I want the press to be interested in the kind of music I make, not that I spent a day out with Carston Hewlett."

"And a night too." Charlie chuckled evilly. "But I'm just preparing you for the kind of interrogation you'll be facing. One journalist asked me this very leading question."

"What very leading question?"

"If you and Mister Playwright organized the whole thing to drum up interest in the festival and the arts in general. And in yourselves. So your names are linked together in the gossip columns because you have other plans."

She raised her eyebrows. "Plans?"

"Career plans. Movie plans. Television plans."

Sherry felt faintly ill. "Damn!"

"Just letting you know which way the wind's blowing, chicken. But I know you can handle nosy questions; you're pretty good at that kind of thing. There's a cocktail and press conference down in the dining room, and I want you down there looking like a princess in twenty-nine minutes flat."

"I'll tell you what sort of a princess I'll look like: like the one who tried to sleep with a football-sized pea under her straw mattress." There were dark circles under her eyes, and she didn't feel like covering them over with goop either. If Carston liked her without makeup, she'd go easy on the stuff, no matter what Charlie and her fans said about it. She wouldn't mind getting out of spangled costumes for a while either. Looking normal, or elegant. Buying a simple, black dress and surprising Carston with understatement.

"And I haven't even told you about the phone call yet."

"Phone call?" She wheeled around, watched Charlie with foreboding. He was looking even smugger than usual: the cat who'd swallowed a vulture whole. Why hadn't she noticed? "What phone call?"

"You're going to like this."

"You sure?"

"Of course I am. You've been making my life miserable for over a year now about this very thing. The call was from Hollywood. From Mark Ballance."

"The director?"

"You got it. The director. Chicken, you've gotten your first big acting break. I've wangled a role for you in Ballance's *Baby and the Bank*."

"The television series? I'm being hired as an actress?" Sherry couldn't believe her ears. Finally. She was getting a break. Then, just as quickly, her heart plummeted. "In *Baby and the Bank*?"

"Okay, okay." Charlie waved his stubby hand. "It's not a great series, I'll give you that. But the public loves it, and it's a big step in. Your first. I couldn't get you a leading role in some big film just like that, you know. Gotta start smallish. But that's not all either. You know who showed up here in Midville this morning? Ned Lantini. You know? Lantini. The producer, right? I've spent hours chewing the fat with him, selling you as an actress. He wants you to take a look at one of his scripts: a science fiction thriller about a serial killer."

"How awful." She grimaced.

"As I said, gotta start somewhere. Small is good. Besides, you're no young starlet. You're coming into this late in the game. Let's take what we can get at first."

"Oh Charlie..." How was it possible to feel so miserable?

"Now what's the matter?" Charlie looked genuinely puzzled. "I thought you'd be jumping in the air with joy. I get you where you want to go, and here you are, looking miserable."

She sighed. "Why is life so unfair?"

Charlie sat there silently for a minute or two, the wheels in his head churning slowly before coming up with Bingo. "This lack of enthusiasm on your part, does it, by any chance, have something to do with Hewlett? Him being a playwright and all?"

"Yes." She swallowed. "You see, he's ultra-sensitive about people using others to get what they want. And now, if he thinks I'm headed for an acting career he might just take it the wrong way."

Charlie nodded thoughtfully. "Maybe he will," he said slowly. "Maybe he won't. But if you like him and he likes you, all you have to do is explain. He's bright enough to handle facts, isn't he? And if he isn't, why ruin your chances of doing something you've always wanted just because Mr. Ivy League is hypersensitive? Besides, what does Hollywood have to do with live theater? Nothing. Especially not a lousy television series like *Baby and the Bank* or one of Lantini's tenth-rate sci-fi flicks."

Sherry didn't feel as though she had enough humor left over for a snigger.

Chapter Seven

Lila Patterson lay across the large couch in Carston's hotel room. Her legs in their tight black pants and high black boots were long and elegant, and when she stretched, oh so languorously, she knew her supple, slender body was shown to best advantage.

Sitting across from her, Carston tensely drummed his fingers on the arm of his chair. He'd noticed the stretch, was well aware of Lila's seductive powers. He always had been. She was a beautiful woman and a very talented actress, but that didn't mean they had to fall into each other's arms. He wasn't in the least bit interested in being another one of Lila's conquests. If he had one fast rule, it was keep personal relationships separate from working ones—and that was something he hadn't been smart enough to do in his younger days. He'd paid the price for that foolishness too, and he wasn't about to repeat the same idiotic experience now.

These days, his emotions came equipped with a very effective on/off switch. Well...he thought they did. So why did he only want to see Sherry again? To be standing beside her and watching her smile up at him, to be hearing one of her funny quips? And why the hell was he so damn intrigued by her?

Temporary lust, he told himself. Again. Nothing more than lust. And this impatience was no more than an adolescent manifestation of those same lusty feelings. When this festival was over, he and Sherry would go their separate ways, calmly, intelligently, knowing the good memories were quite enough. Because Sherry was a woman of the world; she knew better than to become attached to a man she'd had a brief fling with. She did know that, didn't she? Of course. And if not, well, that was her problem. Nothing to do with him.

"So where have you and the country star been holing out?" Lila's voice held more than a hint of mockery.

Or was it jealousy? Lila always needed to be number one: in the limelight onstage and off. "We weren't holing out. I told you that. We spent the night in a cold wet barn surrounded by a troop of boy scouts and an army of spiders."

Lila's tinkle of laughter contained no humor. "And when will your new play be ready?"

"What new play would that be?" He was getting tired of the insinuations. He and Sherry had shared twenty-four hours of light-hearted fun. Just that and nothing more. Why did Lila want to ruin something so innocent?

"The play starring the country music singer. Or is this still under wraps?"

"Is what under wraps? Why the hell would I put Sherry Valentine into one of my plays? She's a singer. As far as I know, I don't write musicals."

Why was it suddenly so important for everyone to know what he did—and with whom—in his free time? Of course, Sherry had warned him about this very thing; she'd also told him how damaging publicity and gossip were. So he'd keep a cool head, not let things go too far.

"Okay." Lila shrugged her lovely shoulders. "Play innocent if you want. I just thought I'd let you know what people are saying."

"You haven't let me *know* anything so far," Carston said more heatedly than he'd intended. "You're just *hinting*, as far as I can tell."

"Okay. You want facts? Here's one." Lila's violet eyes met his squarely. "Sherry Valentine's agent or manager—whatever you call him—has just spent almost the whole day with Ned Lantini. Well, almost the whole day." Lila smirked. "Minus the times Lantini tried to get me alone so he could rub up against me."

"Lantini? The producer of science fiction trash?"

Lila nodded. "The same."

Carston rolled his eyes. "Martian invaders who kidnap women and exploit them in porno flicks."

Lila nodded smugly. "Or carnivorous mushrooms that raise humans for meat."

"Okay, fine." He still didn't see where the conversation was going. "We've got the guy pegged. What does this have to do with Sherry? Aside from the fact that Charlie Bacon and Ned Lantini apparently have a lot to say to each other."

Lila leaned forward, her eyes glowing with unfeigned satisfaction. "Word is, they were conducting business. Word is, Sherry Valentine's aiming for an acting career. Has been for quite some time now. Apparently she's tired of being just a singer. And Lantini just might put Sherry Valentine in one of his films."

Carston stared at her wordlessly for a minute, not certain he'd heard correctly. "In one of Lantini's pieces of junk?" No, this was one rumor he couldn't believe. Would Sherry agree to something so ridiculous? Maybe...How well did he know her after all? Not well at all.

Then the full implication of what Lila had said hit him. Sherry wanted to be an actress? She hadn't said a word about that to him. Why not? Is that why she'd agreed to go off with him? Is that what their so-called relationship was all about? Because she needed contacts in the acting world, she'd homed in on him, the perfect sitting duck?

No, he couldn't believe this was happening. Not again. He stared at Lila. Her smile made him think of a large tiger.

She leaned forward, stretched out one hand, let her long fingers slide along his thigh in a slow caress. "Carston? Why waste your time on an over-age wannabe actress when there's much better around?"

****

The crowd at the press conference was so thick it was impossible to see where Carston was—or if he was there at all. Even the boys in Sherry's band were invisible. Charlie was less of a problem, of course. Here he was, breathing down her neck as usual. Managing her life, killing off independence.

"You look great, chicken. Great but worried. What's bothering you?"

"Where's Carston?"

Charlie smirked. "That bad, is it? You were with him little over two hours ago. What's the rush?"

"I want to know if the gossips have got to him yet or if *Star* has had a go at him. He's not used to smutty publicity."

"Carston's a big boy, chicken. He can take care of himself."

Of course he could. Carston had also been in the limelight for years. But that didn't quash her feeling of dread. She knew she had to get to him fast, explain away any rumors he might have heard. Her eyes roved over the crowd, but she still couldn't find him. Then a cluster of journalists surrounded her, began asking about her concert, and there wasn't any more time to search.

"Will we be hearing new songs here in Midville, or are you sticking to your classics?"

Dutifully, she answered their questions. Soon enough everyone would start moving over to the hors d'oeuvres and begin chowing down. She'd be forgotten…for a while, anyway.

Just then she caught sight of him, standing by the large windows leading to the terrace and talking to a woman with a microphone in her hand. Another journalist. Instantly, her pulse started pounding. How incredibly sexy he was. And rugged. That Harris tweed jacket emphasized his tight, lean body, and his wonderful mouth was crooked into a faintly sardonic but totally delicious half-smile. And how out of place he looked in this impersonal banquet room. He should be standing in the woods, or braced against a turbulent sky. And she'd like to be there too, right beside him, her fingers linked through his, just the way they had been so many times in the last twenty-four hours.

Over the distance separating them, Sherry could almost feel his warmth, smell the soapy male scent of his skin, and a desperate hunger charged through her veins. Again. She was absolutely lusting after the man.

And if those boy scouts hadn't showed up last night...She cut the turbulent thoughts short.

As soon as she could free herself, she cut through the crowd, heading directly toward him, a pin locked into a magnet's power. But when she was only a few feet away, she heard what the journalist was asking. Desire reeled out of the picture.

"And will Sherry Valentine be appearing in your next play?"

Still leaning casually against the window frame, Carston didn't look in the least perturbed. "I never know who will be in plays I haven't yet written."

"But the two of you will be working together in the future?"

"In what way? Sherry's a singer, not an actress."

He even looked bored, Sherry thought. So why was she feeling so anguished? Should she cut in to the interview before the journalist came up with something ridiculous or compromising? Something that would give Carston the wrong idea. At the very least, she could clarify things first—things like the role she was being offered in the television series. Sherry crossed the space separating them.

"Carston—" she began.

But the journalist, ignoring her presence, continued on relentlessly. "Surely you know about Sherry Valentine's plans to become an actress?"

"I do?" he asked calmly.

"She's joining the cast of *Baby and the Bank*. Surely you know that. And since you, a playwright, are the new man in her life, it's normal that—"

"Normal?" His mouth tightened; one eyebrow arched. He turned slightly, and his eyes met Sherry's.

She swallowed. He'd known she was there the whole time. He hadn't denied he was the "man in her life" had he? But he was furious with her, she could see that instantly.

He held her gaze. "Since Ms. Valentine is standing right here, you can ask her if that's what she has in mind."

Titillated, the journalist finally turned to Sherry. "Tell me, Ms. Valentine, how long have you and Carston Hewlett been collaborating?"

"We haven't been collaborating," said Sherry coolly. "I've been planning to work in television for some time now, long before Mr. Hewlett and I met. And there's a great deal of difference between acting in a sitcom and being in the sort of play Mr. Hewlett writes for live theater."

"Isn't that the whole point of the Midville Culture Festival?" gurgled the journalist. "Bringing people together so they can climb to the top of their profession?"

It didn't matter what she said, Sherry thought. She could deny everything, but who'd believe her? Rumors linking her to a famous playwright were just too juicy. And what about Carston? Did he also believe she expected to be put into one of his plays? If his chilly exterior was anything to go by, he probably did. She had to get him alone, try to explain. He had to know he could trust her.

The journalist had turned back to Carston, was questioning him about the play he was presenting in Midville. He answered quietly, precisely, never glancing in Sherry's direction. *As if I'm invisible,* she thought miserably. *Or someone he's never met before in his life*. But she stayed. Who knew when they'd have another opportunity to talk? Or if he even wanted to talk to her?

Only when the finally journalist departed, did Carston's eyes finally meet hers. But there was no complicity there now and no tenderness.

"You're angry with me," Sherry began. "But this is exactly what I warned you about. Remember?"

A cynical smile floated across his lips. "You did indeed warn me about gossip and publicity. But don't you think you could also have mentioned your new career plans? We had enough time together for that to have come up in conversation."

"Oh, come on. You were so quick to accuse me of using Bobby Blake to get where I wanted in the music world. If I'd mentioned acting, you'd have thought the worst of me."

"Maybe." He nodded slowly. "And maybe not. But you could have broached the subject."

She shook her head in denial. "No, you wouldn't have believed me. Look how you're judging me now."

"Judging? Is that what you call it?" Carston's eyebrows rose mockingly. "Or am I just finding out the truth?"

Sherry sighed. What was the point of protesting? Why try convincing him of anything? He'd obviously made up his mind. If she said more, it would sound like begging—begging him to believe and trust her. Why bother? He'd closed his heart.

"Okay. I give up. Think the worst of me."

His hand caught her arm just before she could step away. "It's not the first time it's happened, you see. My ex-wife, Cynthia Preston, pulled the same trick."

Her eyes searched his face. "You were married to Cynthia Preston? The actress?"

He nodded. "Very briefly. And a very long time ago. Cynthia found it convenient to marry a playwright. She was a beautiful woman—she still is. Back then, she was at the peak of her modeling career, and thought the time was right to get into acting. She met me. I was young, inexperienced, a mere puppy. But I was flattered because I believed she loved me."

"She didn't? Silly woman." Sherry had already guessed there was a story like this somewhere in his past, but what did it have to do with her? They'd only known each other for a few days, but hadn't he understood the kind of person she was?

"I'd just won the Wilson award back then. Suddenly I was the young new playwright everyone was talking about. Cynthia zoomed in, programmed me as her personal writer, the one who'd shoot her to fame. So I created a starring role for her; I even believed we were a winning team. That was my first experience of 'love' in the theater world."

"Meaning?"

"Meaning, it meant nothing. We married, became the most talked about theater couple of the year...until I found out Cynthia was having a very passionate affair."

"Things like that do happen," said Sherry quietly.

"They certainly do." His smile was glacial. "When I confronted her, she laughed at my naïveté. Because this affair didn't just 'happen.' Her lover was a man she'd been with for years before meeting me—an unknown actor married to a wealthy woman. Cynthia had decided I'd make her famous, then she'd divorce me, he'd divorce his wife, and they'd live happily ever

103

after."

"And did they?" Sherry asked faintly.

"No. But she managed to attach herself to a successful producer who was far more important for her career aspirations. And, believe me, Cynthia wasn't the only person I've met whose ambition devoured their principles. So, you can understand why I'm not willing to wander into that nasty old labyrinth once again."

Sherry stared at him. He was being unfair. She wasn't Cynthia Preston, and she'd never thought of using Carston.

Then unhappiness dissipated, became anger. Why feel like a victim? And if he tagged her as a vulture, well, she could live with that too. There was something else going on here. She knew it. And it had nothing to do with acting, actresses or ambition.

She raised her chin, kept her voice even. "You know what I think? I think something happened when we met. Not just desire. Something else too. Something that makes you *feel*. But you don't want that. So, to protect yourself, you're looking for flaws. Something to burst the pretty bubble and turn me into a monster. That way you can go back to your country hideaway and never regret anything."

His expression was inscrutable.

She turned and walked away. Leaving him standing there. With his pride, his suspicions, and all his wrong ideas.

****

Hidden by the darkness, Sherry sat in the back row of the theater watching the rehearsal of Carston's play. Sure, she felt like a spy, even a stalker, but she was only sticking to their agreement. Even if, as far as he was concerned, it had been canceled.

She saw Carston up front, sitting in the second row. He never once looked behind him, so he never knew she was there. Of course, she didn't approach him. Why court rejection? *Damn him and his lousy suspicions.* Sherry didn't know if she was angrier with all the gossip-mongering journalists in the world or just with Carston. And why fret about such a person anyway? Her one big mistake had been to let down her defenses with a man who couldn't do the same. He'd have doubted her sincerity no matter what she'd said. And if something tender and delicate had once existed between them, it was definitely over.

She shook her head, ordered herself to stop being melodramatic. What had really happened? They'd shared a few kisses, a few caresses, and had momentarily been carried away by one thing: raw desire. Had she really thought this was the beginning of a love story? Nonsense! Love happened between two people who cared about each another. Love was mutual. What she'd experienced with Carston had been a one-sided proposition. An obsession.

"Cut this out!" she muttered to herself. "You're sitting here because you want to see his play, see how a rehearsal goes, see top-notch actors work. You're here to learn." She forced herself to concentrate on the action onstage. One thing couldn't be denied: Lila Patterson was stunning. Tall and slender yet imposing, her curling black hair framed a perfect oval face, and those violet-blue eyes could be seen from all the way back here, in the last row. She was also an excellent actress—every gesture, every movement, every inflection in her voice was controlled.

The play was brilliant too, like all of Carston's work. The interaction of the three actors on stage, the subtle web of words, thrilled Sherry. Yes, this was why she loved the theater. This was why she'd always read plays, gone to see them every chance she got. She'd wanted for so long to be part of this magic—magic that probably had very little to do with the *Baby and the Bank* production.

Still, as Charlie had pointed out, she had to start somewhere. But she couldn't help wondering if Lila Patterson had ever needed to act in a tacky sitcom. She doubted it.

The rehearsal came to an end. Carston leapt up from his seat, went backstage. Time for Sherry to make a move. Get out of here. She'd miss the final performance in two days time. Tomorrow evening she'd be giving her own concert; after that, she'd hit the road with Charlie and her boys. If there'd been a good reason to stay on in Midville, she'd have done it. But now there wasn't. Not any more. Hanging on would be painful, and Carston would probably just ignore her anytime their paths crossed.

As for that romantic candlelit dinner, it was never, ever, going to happen.

Chapter Eight

She felt Charlie's eyes on her when Carston appeared in the breakfast room, Lila Patterson by his side. They might as well have staggered into the room naked, thought Sherry bitterly. It couldn't have been clearer to her—or to anyone else watching them—they'd spent the night together, probably making passionate love. Phooey on them both. And best wishes. So much for Carston's supposed allergy to theater romance.

As for her boys, they were on good behavior at the moment, pretending to concentrate on eating breakfast, probably to spare her feelings. Which made matters worse, somehow. She couldn't stand their cautious show of loyalty one minute more, even though she knew everyone meant well. Forcing herself to smile, she raised one eyebrow with unconcern.

"Cute couple," she said calmly. After all, someone needed to break the strained silence around the table. She might as well be the one to do it.

"Oh yeah?" Charlie observed the couple across the room, thoughtfully. Then shrugged. "They don't seem so cute to me. Just watch them. Patterson look happy to you? Like a woman with a guy who's madly in love with her? When she glanced this way a second ago and saw you—well, chicken, if looks could kill, you'd be a roast."

"Oh please, Charlie." Sherry shrugged with fake indifference and nonchalantly reached for another piece of toast, determined to show her appetite was undiminished. "How could Lila Patterson think I'm a rival if I'm not even playing the game?"

"Good for you then. Keep away from the guy. If the big romance between you and Hewlett is over just because you're moving into the acting scene, that makes him a write-off in my books."

"I can't believe we're going over the same old ground again," said Sherry, exasperated. "There was no big romance between Carston and myself. We went out for dinner one night. We got stuck in a barn another night and—"

"Yeah, yeah, yeah," Charlie grunted. "I know the whole story backwards. So tell me, you go see his rehearsal last night?"

"I did. And the play was very interesting," she answered primly, and began buttering the cold toast she had no desire to eat.

"So if there's no reason to carry on with your deal, why'd you bother going?"

"Because that's the way I am. I'm not going to be scared off by rude behavior. Besides, I really did want to see his play. See some real acting."

Charlie put down his fork and knife. Leaned back, pulled the morning's first smelly unlit cigar out of his pocket. "You want my advice?"

"No, but you'll give it to me anyway. As usual. Anyone can see you coming from light years away."

"Forget him. The world is chock full of these overly sensitive creative types who'd accuse their own grandmothers of plotting behind their back. If that's how Hewlett functions, you'd waste a lifetime trying to convince him you're sincere. He'd never believe you."

"You're really something, Charlie. One minute you're trying to create a romance, and the next, you're calling off the dogs."

Charlie grunted, a sound that could have meant pretty well anything. Or nothing. "Let's drop the subject. Ned Lantini just walked into the dining room, and he's headed in this direction. I'm trying to convince the guy he has a script for you to look at. So be nice." He looked at the boys and jabbed his cigar in their direction. "As for you guys, you all stick around the hotel. This afternoon, we're going over to the hall to prepare tonight's concert."

He turned back to Sherry. "And I repeat my advice: keep away from Hewlett. You don't need problems. Tomorrow, we'll be hundreds of miles away, and he'll be nothing more than a bad memory."

It was clear Charlie would do his best to make sure things happened that way too.

****

When she was performing, making music, nothing else mattered to her, that much was evident to Carston. And since the audience expected the best of Sherry Valentine, she gave it to them. It was exciting music: old traditional sounds were blended into newer ones. And Sherry was a determined, precise, and talented woman working in tandem with her top-notch boys.

Never again would he be stupid enough to doubt the importance of her work. Through pure ignorance, he'd underestimated her. Never nasal, never harsh, the remarkable purity of her voice went arrow-straight into his heart.

He was proud of her. Proud that, only two nights ago, he'd held her in his arms. That he knew the subtle perfume of her hair, her skin. The warm response of her mouth. Onstage, the white boots and white jeans set off the length of her legs to perfection; the fringed and sequined blouse displayed her soft curves. She was utterly beautiful.

She didn't know he was out here, of course. How could she? Sure, he'd reacted badly to the news that Sherry was moving into an acting career. He'd felt betrayed. Why hadn't she confided in him? Had he really believed she'd wanted to use him? Really? Well, perhaps she did expect something: an introduction to people who'd help her get started. But, so what? He also remembered Sherry's generosity at the hospital, her incredible good nature when forced to tramp miles in a storm and spend the night in a chilly barn. He'd enjoyed being with her. Very much.

And she'd been right: he did care. More than he wanted to, more than felt comfortable. And that frightened him. Yes, he was an emotional coward, but he didn't want to be. He was also a total jerk. He'd acted badly; he'd put their budding relationship into jeopardy. And he'd even shown her what an idiot he was.

Why had he let himself get worked up by a journalist? By Lila Patterson? His stupid reaction had cost him time. He could have been spending it with Sherry instead.

He'd gone down in her esteem too. In the breakfast room this morning, he'd seen her with Charlie and her boys, seen how they'd noticed him crossing the room with Lila. Sherry's eyes had been mocking. She probably thought he and Lila were lovers, that they'd spent a wild night together. But they hadn't.

He needed to talk to Sherry. He'd do it tonight, just as soon as this show was over.

****

The whole world seemed to be backstage: journalists, festival sponsors, local businessmen, politicians, and the odd fan who'd somehow managed to sneak past the guards. One man, tall, dark, and handsome, presented Sherry with a huge bouquet of flowers, and Carston saw how she smiled at him. Who the hell was he? Why was she smiling like that? And why the hell hadn't *he* thought about bringing her flowers? Red roses, for example.

Carston fought through the crowd, trying to get closer, pushing against the mayor who still managed to clap him enthusiastically on the shoulder. He didn't even mind. Not at the moment.

"Great concert, huh," the mayor roared over the din. He looked chuffed, as if personally responsible for the success.

"I'm trying to tell Sherry just that," said Carston as he elbowed another half-inch forward.

The mayor chuckled. "Looks like she's plenty tied up at the moment."

Carston almost growled. "Who's the guy she's talking to?"

"Todd Barclay. Local oil man."

An oil man? Here in Midville? And what right did he, Carston, have to feel jealous?

He watched Sherry receiving compliments and congratulations; she did it with grace, although she must be exhausted. Charlie Bacon never left her side, of course, sticking to her like a pilot fish its shark. Carston was fairly certain Charlie had seen him too, but hadn't acknowledged his presence. No cheery hello tonight. No waving him over. If Sherry felt the same way, he was out of luck.

He saw Todd Barclay glow down at Sherry, his smile full of innuendo. "Will I have the honor of your company at a late supper this evening?"

She did seem to do that to males, Carston thought sourly. Had them drooling without making so much as a personal gesture. And *he* was the one she should be dining with, not oily Todd.

"No can do, Mr. Barclay," Charlie's voice cut in smoothly. "Miss Valentine, the boys, and I are booked for a midnight dinner celebration at the hotel."

Thank goodness for Charlie, Carston thought. He didn't like the look of the oil magnate one bit, and he felt a primitive need to intervene, pull Sherry away, tell everyone she was his.

Charlie's eyes flickered in Carston's direction, only for a brief second, but it was long enough to show how superfluous he considered him. Then he looked back at the oil man. "Of course, Mr. Barclay, you're more than welcome to join us, isn't that right, Sherry?"

"More than happy to do just that," Todd Barclay answered suavely.

Carston pushed his way closer. "Sherry?"

She turned slightly. Saw him. Her impersonal smile vanished, was replaced by something else altogether. Her mouth softened, her eyes showed warmth. And hope, perhaps? Vulnerability? She was pleased to see him, he knew it. Rudely, he elbowed closer still until he was beside her.

"You came to the concert after all." Her voice, soft, enticing, was meant only for him.

"You were wonderful."

"Thank you," she answered simply.

He wanted to say more, of course. Much more. Even more powerful was the urge to reach out, pull her into his arms. But he couldn't do that either. Not yet.

"Sherry—" he began.

But a massive shoulder suddenly separated him from her, and further conversation was squashed under the weight of Charlie's loud bellow. "Sherry? Look who's here to meet you: Ralph Reckon." An elegant, dissipated-looking gray-haired man was tugged into the picture.

Ralph Reckon: Hollywood actor. Okay, a big name, but a lousy actor and a womanizer, Carston knew that for a fact. He watched Ralph Reckon pick up Sherry's free hand, kiss it—a trick he'd perfected in all the gory crusader films he'd starred in over the years.

"Charmed, Ms. Valentine." Reckon's implants gleamed ultra-white. "And you'll soon be joining us in Hollywood. *Baby and the Bank*, am I right?"

"Yes." Sherry didn't look wildly enthusiastic.

"Perhaps you'll let me be your guide when you arrive in Los Angeles?"

Guide? Yeah sure. Carston knew all about the sort of guidance Reckon was referring to.

"Forget about *Baby and the Bank*," said another voice. "Sherry and me got bigger plans than that." He saw producer Ned Lantini hove into view. Lantini? That guy was so lecherous, he made Ralph Reckon look like Snow White.

Carston made a move to shoulder his way past

Charlie—shouldering was a technique two could use—but he didn't stand a chance.

His huge paw on Sherry's shoulder, Charlie almost manhandled her away. "Come on, chicken. Let's make a move." And they, the boys, the oily oil man, Lantini, Reckon, the journalists, and hangers-on, began shifting toward the exit.

Carston gave up the fight, refusing to join that particular pack of jackals. Charlie had made him feel perfectly invisible, cut off and cut out. Okay. But at least he knew what the rules of the game were now. Charlie would make sure he and Sherry had no private conversation; he'd managed that very skillfully this time. But Charlie wouldn't be calling *all* the shots. No way.

Carston watched the technicians packing away equipment, coiling up cords and wires.

"Tomorrow is another day," he muttered to himself. "Or so they say."

****

Carston and his mattress hated each other. He tossed, turned, pounded. The mattress retaliated, bouncing back unperturbed. Did he manage to sleep at all? He didn't know and didn't much care. He tried convincing himself that the reason he couldn't stop thinking about Sherry was because of frustrated desire, but even he knew that wasn't true—or, at least, it wasn't entirely true. He'd have been happy just talking to her, hearing her voice, her laughter, sitting across the table from her in a booth in the Paradise Café in Traverton and drinking lousy coffee.

The desire to reach for the telephone beside his bed, call her room, was almost overwhelming. But he resisted the impulse. This was the middle of the night, and besides, he had to be careful. He was getting too involved, feeling too vulnerable. If he ran after her, she'd probably misinterpret everything. Think he meant their relationship would be long, on-going. But where *could* it go? He still didn't see how their lives could possibly intersect, and he wasn't really sure he'd ever want them to.

He'd wait until morning. Things might be clearer in his head then. He and Sherry could talk, and he'd be able to figure out what was really going on between them...maybe. He'd approach her in the breakfast room, when she was there with her boys and Charlie. Now that her concert was over, she'd be bound to have some free time, and even he could juggle his schedule before tonight's performance. If he suggested that in front of everyone, then Charlie couldn't intervene. If he did, what then? Well, he'd come up with something. Play it by ear. He could manage—wasn't he a man of words? The thought comforted him, and near dawn he managed to doze off.

At seven, he was dressed, downstairs, and crossing the lobby in the direction of the breakfast room. There was no Sherry, no Charlie with his cigar, and none of the boys at their usual table. Of course they weren't there. He was far too early. He'd have to sit this out. Drink coffee until his nerves hummed like the strings on a highly-strung electric guitar.

Eight o'clock. Eight-thirty. Where the hell were they? They usually breakfasted at this hour, so why weren't they all there now, fringes wriggling, spangles gleaming? Had they all decided to sleep late? Rest up from the concert?

He pictured Sherry in her bed, sleeping softly, her curls spread out over the pillow. Her eyes opening slowly, just the way they had that morning in the barn. And the way they'd softened when she'd seen him over near the fire? Softness like that had nothing to do with play-acting. No way. What he wouldn't have given to have spent last night beside her. But that hadn't happened. So all he could do now was sit tight, drink more coffee, try and eat something. Sherry would show up sooner or later.

But the waiting game was killing him. Carston stood, left the breakfast room, strode over to the reception desk. The receptionist looked up at him with a coy smile and batted her eyelashes.

"Good morning, Mr. Hewlett. What can I do for you?" Her voice was lazily flirtatious.

Forget about flirting, this was serious. "I'd like the number of Ms. Sherry Valentine's room."

The receptionist stopped batting her eyelashes. "Sherry Valentine? She checked out this morning."

"Checked out?" He stared, not believing his ears. "What do you mean she checked out?"

The receptionist looked at him strangely. "You know. Checked out. Left Midville. Ms. Valentine, her road manager, and her band. At six o'clock this morning."

"Oh." It was all Carston could come up with.

She shrugged. "That's what a musician's life is all about, isn't it? Thank goodness the rest of us don't have to keep up with that kind of schedule. I'm such a lazy bunny myself. I just love luxuriating in a big, soft bed."

"Where did they go?" Carston knew the question was idiotic, but that was okay. He felt like an idiot.

"Who knows? They didn't leave a forwarding address. Musicians are like that. Here today, gone tomorrow."

Carston turned, left the hotel. Stood staring down the sunny main street as if there were something else to see other than cars roaring through Midville. Okay. As far as Sherry was concerned, he'd fluffed it. There'd be no candlelit dinner, no shared bottle of wine, no steamy nights, no more confidences, and no more confusing emotional turmoil. She'd breezed into his life, then breezed out again. He had no way of contacting her now, no address, no phone number. If he wanted to speak to her, he'd have to get in touch with Charlie and depend on *his* good graces—and he now knew how far those would take him.

So. End of story. The best solution? Forget the whole thing. Stop behaving like a besotted adolescent. He was a man in the prime of life, too old for this sort of emotional fooling around. It was even embarrassing at his age. So why had he let himself be obsessed by Sherry? She'd gone on to pursue other dreams, a life in Hollywood, other men. It was time for him to return to his own world too. Tonight his play was being presented; he'd be the one in the limelight. Tomorrow he'd hit the road. Forget what happened here. Forget Sherry Valentine.

He'd manage that, all right, and he'd do it very well. He knew he would.

Chapter Nine

"Oh, Jed. You couldn't possibly mean that. Take our baby away? No. Oh no, oh no. You couldn't." Samantha, played by actress Judy Dellor, blinked her big, blue eyes. Holding her arms stiffly by her side, she poked her head forward in jerky little gestures meant to imitate an emotion of some sort.

Sherry sighed. Judy Dellor didn't have the faintest idea of how to move in front of a camera, but then again, she didn't have to. She was director Mark Ballance's wife, and just so long as she kept that position, she'd be the long-time star of *Baby and the Bank*.

"What do you mean I couldn't do that?" Jed, played by Tony Taylor, tried to look ferocious...and failed. Sherry sighed again, wondered if even a very small flea would have felt threatened.

"But Jed, I love our baby." Samantha shook her curls in a vague facsimile of frenzy.

"Does that mean I don't?" Jed's voice rose in a squeak.

"Cut!" shouted Mark Ballance. "Okay, Rolanda? Walk into the room like you just heard something that's gonna make you angry."

Samantha's wicked aunt Rolanda (played by Sherry Valentine) got into position; the camera panned in. She prepared to paste the appropriate expression on

118

her face. The clapboard snapped and filming began. Sherry moved forward.

"Cut."

Now the camera moved back to Samantha and Jed. The clapboard snapped, and filming began again.

"Eek," exclaimed Samantha.

"Rolanda! What are you doing here?" growled Jed. For the first time that morning he almost sounded sincere.

"Cut. Back to Rolanda."

The clapboard snapped and filming began again.

"I'm interrupting, I see," Rolanda (aka Sherry) said with what she hoped was just the right suggestion of menace.

"Cut." Director Mark Ballance heaved himself out of his chair. Moved over to the cameraman and technicians to view the results of the last hour's shooting on the screen. Sherry held her breath until she heard him call, "Okay, kids. That's it for today."

"You're going to keep that?" Sherry asked, her voice flat. She was certain she'd just witnessed—and participated in—the worst piece of acting on earth. Acting? No, she couldn't even call it that.

Ballance grunted sourly. "Damn right, I'm gonna keep it. I couldn't go through all that crap again." He turned to his actress wife. "Get ready. You've got five minutes."

Judy blinked mascara black lashes with annoyance. "Five minutes? What is this? A bad joke?" Her baby voice was petulant: she was hardly better at real life drama than acting in front of a camera.

Feeling as frustrated as she usually did after a day's filming, Sherry stalked to the dressing room. She was dying to scrape the makeup off her face: television goop was as bad as the stuff she'd had to wear as a singer. At least there were some advantages: Mark Ballance hadn't protested when she'd shown up at the studio without her curls but with her natural hair color—dull sand, she called it. Sand threaded through with enough pale silver threads to give it a lovely sheen. Thank goodness, she'd always only used temporary color instead of dying it. Now, silky, gently waving, it fell softly to her shoulders. As for her green contact lenses, they'd gone directly into the garbage.

Cleansed of her television makeup, Sherry slipped into a loose print dress and headed out. This was the best part of the day: leaving. But a blast of polluted, exhausted air hit her as soon as she reached the street. No relief in sight. And she was stuck here. In this new career, this new city, this new life.

Stuck? *Come on*, she chided herself. *You chose this*. And yes, parts of California were beautiful. And yes, Hollywood could be an exciting place to live, with concerts, museums, art exhibitions, dance performances, parties, wonderful restaurants, palm trees, exquisite homes, and interesting people who did things. But quite simply, it wasn't the place for her. She couldn't shake off the feeling she'd made a terrible mistake in coming here.

Crossing the pavement just past the exit gate of the studio, she heard someone calling her name. She turned, saw actor Allan Mace waving to her. She waited until he caught up.

"Have time for a drink in the Hole?" he asked. The Hole was the studio bar where actors, extras, and crew mingled happily.

Sherry smiled. "I certainly do. Just as long as we don't run into Jason Reel in there. He's been pressuring me on behalf of Ned Lantini."

Allan laughed. "Ah ha! So Neddy's been trying to get you into his clutches."

"I suppose so. He keeps promising—or should I say threatening?—to put me into one of his films." She couldn't sound enthusiastic if she'd tried.

Allan took her elbow and steered her inside the bar. "Tell me all about it over a glass of white wine."

Allan Mace was certainly a remarkable-looking man Sherry mused—and not for the first time either. Just look at that blond hair flowing over his broad forehead, his straight, perfect nose, those blue eyes, strong jaw, high cheekbones, and perfectly arched eyebrows. His smile revealed the whitest, straightest, most gorgeous teeth in Hollywood, and just under his tight T-shirt and even tighter jeans, muscles rippled and bulged with a life of their own.

In fact, Allan Mace was one of the most gorgeous men she'd ever seen. Allan also thought so: he never could get enough of his own image. If there was a mirror anywhere in the area, he concentrated on watching the way his mouth moved when talking, laughing, or forming different vowel sounds. Going to a restaurant or a bar with Allan meant its walls would be covered with mirrors, and he'd never have time to look her in the eye. Sherry had coped with her share of rivals in her life, but she'd never lost out so completely as she did with him: the great love of Allan Mace's life was Allan Mace.

But she really did enjoy his company. He was witty; he was always in a good mood; he was sympathetic. Never once had he tried to squeeze her, maul her, tell her what she should be doing, or try to convince her they'd make magic together. He was a relief. They'd met on the set of *Baby and the Bank* (he played the role of a wonderfully handsome heartbreaker) and had become great friends immediately.

They carried their glasses of wine to a corner table where Allan could look into the mirror behind Sherry's shoulder and admire how nicely the dim light softened his well-cut features. "So Neddy's considering you for his next blockbuster, *Death Ship*, is he?"

"And not because of my acting ability either."

Allan chuckled. "Of course not. Neddy has never cared about trivial things like acting ability."

"He's only interested because I've never been to bed with him. He doesn't care about me one way or the other, but he can't work out how I can resist his charm. He thinks I should be grateful for the chance to have a role in his production."

"Will you do it eventually?" Allan turned his head slightly to the right, a more flattering angle.

"Do what? Sleep with Lantini or act in his film?"

"Either one."

"Then the answer is no to both. As far as I'm concerned, better dead than Ned."

"You're crazy if you refuse the part. You'd make megabucks."

Sherry looked at him with indignation. "Allan, do you know what the storyline is? It's about a serial killer from another planet. I'm supposed to play the serial killer's former and much older sex playmate—until he chops me into bite-sized tender morsels with a vegetable grinder or something."

"Cute. All of Neddy's films are like that. What do you get to wear?"

"Almost nothing. Or nothing, if Neddy gets his way. Maybe I'll be allowed a filmy pair of underpants. Just before I get turned into coleslaw, Neddy says he wants me topless because the extraterrestrial creep is a breast fetishist. He also says he wants to see me with my clothes off so he can decide if I'm really good for the part." Sherry stopped, quirked one eyebrow. "Hey, Allan, do you think this particular film is Ned's lightly disguised autobiography? I do. Not that I care."

Allan laughed. Then his eyes met Sherry's, and the smile vanished. "You don't really enjoy the Hollywood world, do you?"

"No," she answered slowly. "I don't. Not really."

"Are you sorry you gave up singing?"

She shook her head. "Sorry? Coming out here and getting into acting was something I *had* to do. Otherwise I'd have felt frustrated for the rest of my life simply because I *thought* this was my real vocation."

"And it isn't," Allan said sympathetically.

"It isn't," Sherry confirmed. "Maybe I just tried to do it too late in the game. Maybe I should have tried acting twenty-five or thirty years ago. These days, I don't have the patience or the dedication for television or film. I hate the way scenes are chopped here, cut there. I hate doing every banal little thing over and over again so it can be shot from different angles. Sure, some people love this way of working—you probably do. But I don't. I guess I just wasn't cut out for it. Wrong temperament. Wrong attitude. And no doubt, I'm also lacking in talent."

"Talent only happens when the work you're doing is meaningful to you," said Allan gently. "You didn't doubt your talent when you were singing, did you?"

She shrugged. "Maybe not. But who knows? I'm not sure of anything anymore. Except...as soon as I can, I'm going back to music. If I can wriggle out of my television contract."

As soon as she said the words, she felt slightly stunned: she'd never actually come out and admitted how frustrated she felt. But it was true: she missed her own world. She missed her research, her music. She missed Charlie and all her boys. She missed preparing for concerts. Most of all, she missed the wild excitement of performing in front of a live audience. Yes, she wanted out.

****

Carston quickly glanced to the left, then to the right. Here he was, standing beside the magazine display shelves in the Super Superette in the neighboring village of Humm. On his left, a short man with a bristling moustache perused a fishing magazine. On his right, a young girl with freckles, glasses, and a perfectly blank face, chewed a chocolate bar and read *Star*. Edging in closer, Carston peeked over her shoulder.

FICKLE SHERRY!
NEW ROMANCE WITH ACTOR ALLAN MACE
THIS TIME IT'S FOR REAL, CONFIDES THE STAR

"For real?" Carston muttered sourly. "Who and what's for real? What kind of person goes from one man to another like that?"

For the hundredth time, he told himself how lucky he was that he hadn't allowed himself to become more involved with Sherry. How right he'd been not to contact her again. Yes, his instincts had ensured his survival, all right. So what if he lay awake every single damn night just thinking about her. So what if the memory of the time they'd spent together rolled out in his mind every time he took another woman out for dinner—and he'd done quite a bit of that. He'd had to, as an antidote to Sherry Valentine.

He peered over the freckled girl's shoulder again. There was a photo of Sherry, a different one this time. Something about it looked familiar. Very, very familiar. He moved in closer still. Yes, Sherry was wearing one of her country costumes, but now he thought he recognized the shirt.

Yes, of course he did. He knew that shirt, the jeans, and he even knew where that photo had been taken: in Midville. In the hotel lobby. That blur of brown and beige behind Sherry? Why, he was there in the photo too. He remembered how cameras had flashed when they'd made their entrance after their dinner together in the Blue Lagoon. Strange, they hadn't used a more recent photo.

"You so interested, go get your own copy." The voice, indignant, nasal, pulled him out of his reverie. He found himself staring into the freckled girl's pink-framed glasses. Her hand holding the crumpled chocolate bar wrapper was balled into a fist. "What are you, anyway? Some kinda weirdo or what?"

Humiliated at having been caught out, Carston decided the best defense was attack. Pulling himself up to his full height he announced with as much dignity as he could muster, "I'm shocked that a person of your age reads such trash."

"Hey!" interrupted the man with the fishing magazine. "What's going on here? You some sort of weirdo bothers young girls?" He knit his brows, and his moustache trembled.

Carston noticed the man's resemblance to an *Australopithecus*—and not a particularly nice-looking *Australopithecus*. He probably fished with a pointed stick and ate with a flint.

No amount of explaining would clear up this situation, not with these people, he thought desperately. The best tactic was total retreat. Scraping his remaining dignity together, Carston strode out of the Super Superette. And he hadn't even had a chance to see what Allan Mace looked like.

****

Okay, he was a sneak. He hated doing this, and he hated himself for doing it. But could he stop? No. He couldn't. Carston peeked over the paper rack at the back of Myrtle Ripe's Grocery in Cutter's Edge. Myrtle was busy talking with that gossipy Mrs. Pinch from Gossamer Hill. On his left, a young mother was busy trying to pry plastic sacks of caramels out of the grasping and grubby fingers of two of her offspring. Mr. Ripe, concentrating hard on chewing a piece of gum, was staring out the door and down the road.

In other words, the coast was fairly clear. No one, not one person, was paying the slightest attention to what he, intellectual playwright, full-time resident of Cutter's Edge, was up to. And, since no one was watching him, he could take the leap. Stealthily, he slipped the bright vulgar copy of *Glitzy* off the shelf and began leafing through the pages. It wasn't his fault. Normally, he would never even touch the slick pages of a magazine this tawdry. But today was different. He'd seen the bright red headline smeared across the front page, and he had to know more.

HAPPINESS AT LAST FOR SHERRY VALENTINE AFTER DUMPING NED LANTINI: WEDDING PLANS WITH JASON REEL

Here she was, on page three. It was an old photo—one he'd already seen back in Midville when he'd known her as a country singer. She was laughing into the camera lens, wearing one of her fringed costumes. Just seeing her face again was like being on the receiving end of a punch in the gut. It reminded him of her laughter, the softness and natural scent of her warm skin. How could he forget things like that? The memory of her voice had haunted him for months now.

He stared at the photo. Her mouth. The feel of her lips, he remembered those things too. On the opposite page was a photo of the proud future husband, just another superficial, banal Hollywood face. Carston was scathing. Is that what Sherry really wanted? It must be. He couldn't say he'd known her for very long—they'd only been together for a total of three days—but she hadn't seemed like the sort of person who'd take marriage lightly. Not again. Because she'd already made that mistake twice in her life. Or maybe he was getting things all wrong. If she really was marrying Jason Reel, it must be because she loved him.

The very idea of banal-faced Hollywood pretty-boys like Allan Mace or Jason Reel kissing Sherry, touching her, feeling her beautiful body, seared into Carston's mind, causing immediate painful damage. Why even dwell on such thoughts? It didn't matter to him what she did with her life.

Or did it? How was she feeling now? Hadn't she felt anything for him? He'd thought so. And it had frightened him so much he'd run in the opposite direction. On the other hand, if she really *had* cared for him, how could she be making wedding plans with someone else after such a short time?

"Isn't *Glitzy* wonderful?" burbled an enthusiastic voice on his left. "I just love that magazine too."

Carston turned, appalled. And came face-to-face with Myrtle Ripe. He'd been so involved in looking at Sherry's picture, he hadn't sensed that venerable village gossip creeping up on him.

Humiliated, he slapped the pages shut. This was ridiculous. Here he was, reading something cheap and nasty like *Glitzy*, following the most ridiculous Hollywood scandal stories. He was a fool. Hadn't Sherry told him not to believe anything you read in rags like *Glitzy* or *Star*? Disgusted with himself, he stalked out of Myrtle Ripe's without a backward glance.

Chapter Ten

The last snows had melted; warmer weather finally arrived. Carston sat on the wooden terrace of his house, drink in hand, listening to the mocking call of the cuckoo high in that tree over there, to the woodpeckers, the flycatchers, all those tiny birds he'd fed throughout this long winter, creatures he considered good friends. In just the same way, he welcomed the occasional visits from bears, deer, opossums, porcupines, skunks, and squirrels, his closest neighbors.

If he loved the noisy wildlife in the forest, he equally relished his isolation from the human world. He'd never felt the need for company out here. The crowds, the friends? He saw enough of those when he was working on a production in the city. But he'd never wanted to share this tranquilly beautiful part of his life, or this house where he wrote, dreamed, and where his soul rejoiced in living.

Until now. Because he'd spent so much time thinking of Sherry Valentine over the winter, it was almost as if she'd been here with him. He didn't know why, or how, she'd affected him so deeply. He didn't even know what this sort of obsession was called— unless the old word bewitchment fitted the picture. How many times had he pictured her out here, sitting on the terrace with him, watching the animals he loved, thinking she just might love them too?

Or would she? Wasn't he just imagining a woman who thought the way he did, who wanted the same things? He might be: the human mind did do things like that. If those magazine articles were anything to go by, the Hollywood version of Sherry Valentine had nothing whatsoever to do with his fantasy of her.

There was only one way to find out who the real Sherry was: have her here. Just for a while.

The future? He didn't really care about that at the moment. Why worry? Things would work out or they wouldn't. The most important thing was taking a chance. And to make certain he'd get that chance, he'd put his desires into action.

Sherry Valentine was now about to learn that he, Carston Hewlett, had come up with an offer she couldn't resist. An offer that would feed her ambition—and his as well. Something that just might make them both come up winners.

Something that would also give him a chance to catch up on that candlelit dinner he'd promised her. And taste her delicious mouth again.

****

She'd agreed to meet with Jason Reel at the Green Machine, go on to a party at producer Norton Wilde's with him. But first, Sherry had a twenty-minute drive along the freeway. She hated freeways and certainly wasn't in the mood for Jason or a party. Maybe she could plead a migraine after half an hour or so and go home? Certainly no one would notice.

At least that was the one great advantage of being in Hollywood: she was never in the limelight. There were so many glamorous film stars already vying for the interest of their fans and the press that Sherry, a mere newcomer playing an unglamorous role in a television series, could walk through the streets without fear of autograph hunters or the scandal press. For once. And without her curling red hair, her cowgirl outfit, who connected her with Sherry Valentine, country music star? No one.

Jason Reel, his eyes hidden behind a huge pair of sunglasses, was sipping something coral out of a frosty glass when she arrived at the Green Machine. He looked petulant. For the fifteenth time that day, Sherry sighed. Jason was probably having one of his bad days, and that meant he'd be lousy company. She slid into the booth opposite him. "Hi," she said, and forced herself to sound as chirpy as she possibly could.

Jason grimaced, held up one hand, warding her off. "Careful, Sherry. I'm feeling delicate."

But then again, the horrendously loud, bad music pounding out of the overhead speakers would make a worm woozy, Sherry thought. And the décor, largely comprised of lifebuoys, torn fishnet, and framed pictures of shipwrecks, made her feel seasick.

"Look, Jason, if you're not up to this, why don't we take a rain check." She sent up a little prayer to her fairy goddess. With a good dose of magical intervention, Jason just might agree to call the evening off, and she could escape to the peace and quiet of her apartment, the delight of a good book. Why had she even agreed to come? Were bad decisions going to be the main feature of her life from now on? At the moment, it felt exactly that way.

"No way." Jason shook his head. "I promised Wilde I'd bring you to the party. Do you know what he'd do to me if I didn't?" For a moment, the consequences made him look almost perky. Then, remembering it was a delicate day, he slumped back in his seat.

Sherry knew, very well, that Wilde wanted her at his party for yet another attempt at a hot tussle on the casting couch. Did situations like this still exist? Didn't casting couch seductions only happen to young, inexperienced women who were desperate for fame? Obviously not. They belonged to the bottom end of the market where Wilde's productions scraped the ground. But she knew better than to broach the subject with Jason. Instead she quirked an eyebrow, assumed an air of complete innocence, and asked, "What exactly would he do to you, Jason? Come on, spill the beans."

Jason scowled. "Sherry, please. I'm not in the mood for your particular brand of perverse humor. How do you manage to be so positive and energetic all the time anyway?"

Sherry scrutinized the parts of Jason's face not hidden by sunglasses. "Positive energy bothers you? You'd prefer me to suffer from something? Hay fever perhaps? Or a hangover, depression, herpes, stress, or a negative flashback from one of my previous lives? Well, sorry. Here I am, bright-eyed and bushy-tailed, and getting on your nerves." She smirked. "And you're just jealous."

"Bright eyed and bushy tailed? Do people still use expressions like that?" Jason's moue of disgust was destroying his chic.

"Where I come from, dear old Dog's Pass, they sure do."

"I can't believe I'm hearing this. Dog's Pass?" His disgust increased. "The sordid world of stewed catfish and meat pies, I imagine."

Sherry shook her head, her expression dead pan. "That stuff's for rich folks. The rest of us just go in for tails, ears, and snouts. Nothing like a snout sandwich at six in the morning. Sets you up for the long shift in the opossum cannery."

"Sherry, please."

"Because you're feeling too delicate?"

Jason looked at her suspiciously, and narrowed his eyes. "You won't start in on that opossum cannery stuff at the party tonight, will you? Because if you do…"

"Why not?" Sherry chirped innocently. "Is Norton Wilde delicate too?"

"You know what your problem is?" Jason shook his head wearily. "You don't fit in. No one can even have a normal conversation with you."

"Can't make a silk purse out of an opossum's ear," Sherry quipped. Then sighed. "Actually, I don't really want to fit in here."

"Could have fooled me."

"I'd rather fit into somewhere else. A place that has real trees, for example. Trees surrounded by other trees, all of them pushing out of a forest floor."

"Trees here in California just aren't real enough for you?"

"They're very nice, of course. Always green and luxuriant. But they seem so domesticated, so much like stage scenery. I miss real fields too. Fields that smell like earth and growing things. I want barns, and straw, and fallen leaves, and spiders, and walks, and beautiful silence."

That wasn't all, either. Of course she wanted those things, but she also wanted to share them with a rangy, gray-eyed man. The one she'd fallen in love with all those long months ago. The one with whom she'd first experienced the beauty of mountains, fresh air, and forest floors. She wanted to feel the pressure of his arm around her shoulders. She wanted to be able to touch him, feel his lips on hers. How many times had she wished she could be projected back to that warm, Indian summer day when she and Carston had been together in the forest?

For the rest of her life, she knew she'd associate a love of nature with his memory. Some people have a way of coming into your life, even briefly, and changing it forever, she mused. But what was the point of even thinking about Carston Hewlett and other impossible things. She had to live without him and accept that. No one in the world got everything they wanted no matter how hard they tried.

Besides, if she'd mattered to him at all, he'd have contacted her by now. It would have been easy enough to get her address or her phone number through Charlie. But he hadn't done it. He probably didn't like her very much. Or had decided there was no place for her in his world. Or had totally forgotten her. Or was with someone else. No point in dreaming.

Jason stood. "Well you're in luck, kid. Wait to you see Wilde's place. He has trees, grass, flowers—everything set out all pretty, just the way you want it. And there's a big black heart-shaped swimming pool and glassed-in jogging track with footlights. Everything you fitness freaks need."

Sherry laughed. "A fitness freak? Me? Because I like trees?" But why bother with explanations? Norton Wilde's glassed in jogging track had to be a sight better than the décor at the Green Machine.

****

"Sherry-baby, darling." Norton Wilde pressed his nose into her neck for the fortieth time this evening. "You are gorgeous. Gorgeous. Anyone ever tell you that?" He slid his hand onto her hip.

In another minute, he'd be kneading her like a lump of fresh dough. She knew Wilde's technique, knew he'd perfected it to a fine art—if you could call it that. His particular specialty was an uncanny way of creeping up on women, unnoticed. Until it was too late to avoid being mauled. For the fortieth time, Sherry swirled out of grasping distance.

Wilde looked at her speculatively. Smiled. Not warmly either. "Come on, sweetheart. Life's for fun."

"Exactly the way I feel." Sherry's smile was as frosty as his. Her idea of fun didn't include being manhandled. Did he think she should be feeling grateful for his attentions because there were so many younger glamorous and ambitious starlets to be had for the asking?

"You got intimacy issues, sweetheart? Hope not." His fingers had found her hip again, his nose was moving in the direction of her neck.

Again, Sherry stepped aside. What the hell was she doing here? She certainly wasn't enjoying herself. At all. Almost desperately, her eyes swept the crowded and very sterile designer garden, searching for Jason. Where was he? Why had he abandoned her like this? Probably because he was comfortably ensconced in some dark corner confiding to someone else that he was feeling delicate.

Wilde's voice took on a lower, more seductive

tone. "We have to get together, just the two of us, sweetheart. Talk business."

Would they? Sherry's eyes met Wilde's and suddenly she wanted to tell him that the very last thing that interested her was a role in one of his films. In any film. She opened her mouth to say just that, when a new voice cut into the air.

"Hey, chicken. How's tricks?"

It was a voice so familiar, so welcome, she thought she was dreaming. She spun around.

"Charlie. Oh Charlie." She was incapable of saying more.

"In the flesh."

Could this be really happening? Charlie Bacon right here in Hollywood? Really? Yes, really. That big lug was standing right here, in front of her. She threw her arms around his neck.

"Calm down, chicken." He wrapped his arms around her too, his face apoplectic red. But he also looked very chuffed at the reception he'd just received.

"Charlie?" Sherry drew back, looked at him with wonder. "When did you get into town? How did you know I'd be here tonight?" She hadn't felt this happy in months.

"Because I make it my business to know everything where you're concerned. Besides, Norton's been negotiating about a role for you in his new film, right, Norton?"

"Sherry and I were just getting around to details, Charlie, my boy."

"Pleased to hear that, Norton. So I guess I'll just stick around for a while."

Which was almost all she could have asked for,

Sherry thought. Incredible how much she loved her Charlie, interfering, bossy, infuriating, and nosy old Charlie Bacon.

Even though she knew he wouldn't make things easy for her when she told him she wanted to go back to music. He might even consider her a hopelessly fickle person and a quitter to boot. But that didn't matter. She knew she could win him over. He must miss that old life too. He must.

****

"Well, are you an actress or aren't you?" Charlie roared. "I don't know what's wrong with you. You softening up or something? Hollywood ruined the fighter in you? You disappoint me, chicken. I thought you had guts. I thought you were tough and determined. And look at you. You're nothing but a wimp."

"Stop it! I'm sick and tired of your bullying. I've warned you time and time again: you can't push me around all the time. I have rights too. You might have been my agent for the last eighteen years—and a great agent too, *and* my best friend in the whole entire world—but there are limits. Got that?"

"Yeah, I got it, all right. You've become wishy-washy and scared." Charlie Bacon stopped shouting. Suddenly he looked deflated. And defeated. He shook his head sadly. "Well, that's it. I'm finished. Everything has an end, and this is it."

"Except a sausage," Sherry conceded. She'd also stopped screaming.

"A sausage?

"Which has two."

"Two what?"

"Ends. It's a German saying. Everything has an

end except…oh, forget it." Sherry sighed.

"Just goes to show our contract isn't a sausage. I'm resigning as your agent. I mean it, too. Get yourself somebody else. I'm finished. I'm walking out."

"Just because I refuse to go along with everything you say? Just because of that, you're walking out? Are you crazy? Don't forget yourself, Charlie-boy. You're not talking agent talk now. You're talking slave driver lingo. As my agent you have the right to *propose* things to me, and I have the right to say yes or no."

"You don't have the right to say no to this proposition."

"I do. I just did, and I'll do it again just to prove I have the right. No! Got it?"

"Got it."

"Good!"

"Good-bye." He headed for the door.

"Go to Dog's Pass and rot."

He stopped, turned slightly. "I'm not the one from Dog's Pass. You are."

"So they say." She desperately tried to hide a mad desire to smile. If he knew she was about to burst into wild laughter, he'd really never forgive her.

"You aren't?"

"You walk out of here, you quit being my agent, and I'll never tell you the truth."

"Tough. Not knowing won't kill me." He turned, began moving in the direction of the door again.

"Charlie—do you have any idea what you're asking me to do?"

"Of course I do. What kind of dumb question is that? This is your big chance. You wanna stay here in Hollywood and play in science fiction porn? That's what you want in life? Bull. So here I come, offering you the chance of a lifetime, and you tell me, no. You won't do it."

"Charlie, just listen…"

"I have been listening. I've been listening hard. And I still haven't heard one good reason for your turning the offer down. Aside from being scared, that is. But that, you won't admit."

"The hell I won't. Of course I'm scared. I'll admit it. I'll even repeat it. I'm scared. I'm scared of failure, I'm scared of going in over my head, I'm scared of making a fool of myself—"

He cut her off. "The role of a lifetime. And you turn it down. I can't tell you how disappointed I am."

"Look, Charlie. This is a one-act play you're proposing. A *one*-act, *one*-character play. One person, one leading role. On stage, solo. What if I'm no good? Actually, I already *know* I won't be any good. I'm not a real actress, and this isn't just any old cheap role you're pushing me to take. This is heavy stuff. Carston Hewlett is a brilliant playwright. He's always had the best performers in the country working for him. What will happen when he finds out I'm a dud—especially since I really *am* one? And since there'll be nobody else on stage but me, I'll fluff it and it'll be a disaster."

"Big deal. If you fluff it, if you're a dud, then Carston will admit he made a mistake. And I'll admit I made a mistake. You'll be a flop, the critics will slaughter you, and you won't act in another Carston Hewlett play. So what? It'll all blow over in a month or two. You'll survive, I'll survive, and Carston will hire someone like Lila Patterson as a leading lady in his next play. Everybody's allowed to fail some of the time, you know. But that doesn't mean you are a dud or that you *will* fail. Unless you decide to, of course. Unless you talk yourself into failure."

"Oh, Charlie," Sherry moaned, and clasped her hands in front of her as if in supplication. "I don't know what to do. Carston actually agreed to let me do this? You really spoke to him? He really wants me to play the part of Melissa?"

"Yeah, yeah, yeah."

"You bullied him into doing this, right?"

"No way, I did. This was all his idea."

"Oh, sure. I'm supposed to believe this? Knowing you? Knowing him?"

"Listen, chicken, cut this out. You're not going on Broadway, okay? There's no plan for that yet. Unless this play is a brilliant success and you're great in the role, then—and only then—we'll talk big time. For now, this is a play Carston's written for a theater festival in Brandt. If it doesn't work, it'll stop right there."

"I bet it will," she mumbled bitterly.

"But it should work. Just think. Carston's the one who's directing it. You'll go to his house, you'll stay there with him, and while you're there, you'll be working through the script with him. Together, you'll define the character, the moves. With him, you'll learn the techniques you need. You'll be working in tandem. You see? It can't fail. He won't let it fail. And you'll learn all about what being an actress means."

"Oh help," Sherry squeaked. Took a deep shuddering breath. "I'll be going to stay in his house? His own home?"

"That's right. I'm sure he has very nice guest

accommodations." Charlie allowed himself to snicker for a few brief seconds. "You'll stay with him for the duration of the rehearsal time. Something wrong with that? You're both adults; you can handle being a houseguest for a while, can't you?"

She sincerely hoped she could cope with being in such close proximity to Carston day in and day out. And how would she pretend he was nothing more than a friend? A nice-guy playwright who'd agreed to give her a chance in a starring role? Because Carston was the man she cared for, the man who made her heart turn over. She hoped she could control herself. Not throw herself at him and come out with wild declarations of love as soon as she'd finished one glass of wine. "Exactly where is this house of his?"

"Some place called Cutter's Edge."

"Where on earth is that?"

Charlie sneered evilly. "Down the road apiece from Dog's Pass, I reckon."

"How am I supposed to get there?"

"What kind of a crazy question is that?" Charlie shook his head sadly. "You get into a taxi, go to the airport, get on a plane, and fly to the nearest airport where he'll pick you up. Carston will give us all the details."

"Are you coming along?"

"Why would I? I'm going home to Memphis and May. You'll do fine without me. I'm your agent, remember? Not your chaperone."

"Yes, I see." She felt utterly miserable.

"There's more to this, isn't there?" Charlie asked slyly.

"Yes. I guess so."

"What do you feel about the guy? You still like him? You want to see him? Work with him?"

Not meeting his eye, Sherry stared glumly at the boring beige carpet under her feet that really wasn't worth such close scrutiny.

"I guess...I guess...well..." She swallowed. Took the leap. "I fell in love with the guy."

Charlie grunted but offered no other comment. If Sherry had looked up, she'd have seen a very definite look of satisfaction smearing itself across his face.

Chapter Eleven

Like the perfect zombie in a typical Ned Lantini film, Sherry managed to get herself out to the airport, then sit through the long hours of the flight without being in the least aware of any part of her trip. The gorgeous man with salt and pepper hair sitting beside her sent intense vibrations into her sphere, but her personal wavelength was distorted, and he remained invisible. A baby across the aisle never stopped screeching, but that escaped her notice too.

All she knew was that, somehow, she had to prove herself. She had to show Carston Hewlett that she was worth his trust in her. But why on earth had Carston let Charlie bully him into giving her this role in his new play, *Swan Song*? And for a theater festival? It certainly was an unsolved mystery. Then again, Sherry knew how persuasive Charlie could be when he put his mind to something. Now Carston had become his victim too. Was he already regretting the fact? She'd soon find out. And if she sensed the slightest reluctance on his part, she'd back out immediately. Without Charlie around, the escape door would be wide open.

Clutched in her hand was the manuscript Carston had sent via Charlie. She'd gone over the thing so many times now, the pages were little more than torn and crumpled tissue. Still, she read it again and again, although she pretty well had the whole thing down by heart. This ordeal in front of her was horrible to contemplate. How would she ever have enough courage to open her mouth, say those first lines in Carston's presence? She'd feel like a jerk.

She took a taxi from the airport to Cutter's Edge, not caring how much it cost. She hadn't wanted Carston to pick her up, and she hadn't even let him know when she was arriving. In fact, she hadn't even spoken to him on the phone. The arrangements had gone through Charlie, and he'd only reluctantly agreed to go along with this crazy whim of hers, arriving unexpectedly.

The taxi pulled to a halt in the center of a rather picturesque village

"Here you are. Cutter's Edge," said the driver.

Sherry stared out at the street with amazement. This was where Carston lived? Out here in the boonies? Why, Cutter's Edge could be Traverton. There was a general store, a gas station, a tiny school, and a long main street of wooden frame houses, so pretty, she found herself wishing she lived in one of them. Life had to be warm and rosy inside. Warmer and rosier than hers looked now.

"Now where?" asked the taxi driver.

She stopped dreaming. "Beats me," said Sherry. "The house I'm looking for is called Owl's Nest, but I've never been here in my life. I'll go ask for directions." She opened the car door, strolled across the empty main road, and entered the grocery store.

Myrtle Ripe gave Sherry a long and penetrating up and down before answering. "Owl's Nest, eh? You mean Carston Hewlett's place." She almost looked as though she were about to refuse the information. "You a friend of his or something?" There was no ignoring the lascivious emphasis she'd layered onto the word "friend."

"Sort of."

Myrtle Ripe's eyes flickered knowingly.

If the other inhabitants of Cutter's Edge were half as suspicious as she, Sherry mused, Carston would never need a guard dog: Myrtle Ripe made a pit bull with rabies look adorable. Sherry smiled as sweetly and as innocently as she could. She knew from long experience that nosy folk need a certain amount of gossip in order to keep their wheels greased and their tongues wagging. "I'll be acting in Mr. Hewlett's next play."

"Is that so? My, my."

"If you'll be so kind as to give me the directions—"

"Take the Humm road for about two miles, turn left, then right, then left again toward Whoa. First turning on the right and you're there. Got that?"

"Clear as mud," Sherry muttered. Then thanking Myrtle, she left.

But not before she heard Myrtle sniff and say to another nosy-looking woman who had suddenly popped out from behind the magazine shelf, "Call it acting these days, do they?"

Ten minutes later, after rolling down a long, wooded drive, the taxi pulled to a halt. A sagging sign on a wooden gate read Owl's Nest.

"End of the line," said the driver.

Sherry stepped out. So this was it. Ahead of her, cupped into the curve of a hill, was a long, low house of wood and stone, surrounded by vegetation and half hidden by climbing vines. Clearly the place had been designed by an architect who admired Frank Lloyd Wright...unless...was it possible? Was this an original Wright?

"You going to be all right, missus?" The taxi driver was gaping at her curiously. Sherry had totally forgotten him.

"Yes, of course I will be." She wasn't really so sure of that. Only a mid-sea confrontation with a starving shark would have made her feel more anguished. But she wasn't about to pour out her heart to a total stranger, was she? Despite the feeling that her knees were melting, she managed to pay the driver and refuse his offer to carry her bags. No, she wanted to do this slowly. Creep up on the situation. She headed, very slowly, in the direction of what might be the front door.

There was even a doorbell. She pushed the button and waited. What if he wasn't home? Okay, what then? Since he'd only given her the part because Charlie had bullied him into it, what if he was now regretting his decision? What if he was in there with another woman? What if he opened the door and looked at her in that cold, terrible way again?

She could handle the first three scenarios, but not this last one.

She heard the unmistakable sound of a lock being turned, and the door swung open.

And she was face to face with Carston.

Well! Forget all those Hollywood pretty-boys. Look at those laugh lines radiating out from his wonderful gray eyes, the errant curl brushing his forehead. Here was the beautiful impatient mouth, so sensual; she ached with the sudden remembrance of how it had felt to be kissed, wonderfully and deeply, by him. He wore a dark blue sweater, faded tight jeans, and the tall muscular strength of his body pushed at the fabric. Oh, how she'd missed him.

And you are absolutely, hopelessly a goner, said the little warning voice in the back of her mind. Who needed voices? Just being in Carston's presence told her that reality was stronger, far more intense than memory had ever been.

Carston stared down at the woman standing in front of him. It was almost like looking at someone he didn't yet know, except the strong pull of his gut told him otherwise. Yes, it was Sherry Valentine, but this Sherry in front of him was an unknown quantity. Her pale hair, pulled back from her high cheekbones by two simple barrettes, fell in wavy, shimmering simplicity to her shoulders; her fine, almond-shaped, hazel eyes—not bright green—watched him with amusement and not a little mockery. A thin, cotton Indian print dress fell softly, revealing, yet hiding, the rounded curves of her body and, instead of cowboy boots, she wore elegant beige heels. This Sherry was refined, cool. Very different. And still so very desirable.

"Hi."

That voice. Unmistakable: soft, throaty, rich. Only Sherry Valentine had a voice like that. She was observing him, waiting for a sign, an emotion.

Unable to move, he could only stare with wonder. "You've changed so much." He managed to say, and shook his head in disbelief.

"This is the real Sherry." She smiled faintly. "The one that was hidden under all the makeup and curled dyed hair. No more green contact lenses for that magic cat look, either. And no cowgirl fringes, no sparkles."

147

The smile vanished and she looked at him questioningly. "I guess you don't watch that awful television series *Baby and the Bank*. I mean, you didn't miss anything...but you'd have seen how I look now."

"I don't own a television."

She raised her eyebrows. "Welcome to Cutter's Edge and the fourteenth century?"

He felt idiotic. "It never dawned on me to go somewhere and watch the series," he said honestly. That would have been so easy to do too. He hadn't needed to sneak around peeking at *Star* or *Glitzy*.

She shrugged. "Well, here I am anyway. Just basic Sherry Valentine. I hope you don't mind." She sounded bright, flippant. Or just defensive. And she must still be waiting for some sort of a reaction from him.

Or perhaps she was sorry she was here? That he'd forced her hand. When Charlie had told him how hard it had been to convince her to take up his offer of a starring role in his play, he'd hardly been able to believe his ears. Hard? Why? Wasn't it everything she'd wanted?

And here he was, staring at her, taking her in. The space separating them seemed enormous, a vast universe that had to be negotiated somehow. Yet every inch of his body ached with the desire to feel her warmth, her weight against him, her arms around him. He wasn't even aware that he was still standing in the doorway. That she was still outside, on the landing, a vision traced in gold by the late afternoon sunshine.

Reaching out timidly, he softly touched her shining, silky hair with his fingertips.

"You are very beautiful as basic Sherry Valentine," he said simply. "And I can't even begin to tell you how happy I am to see you again."

Her eyes softened with pleasure. She swallowed. "Ditto," she said softly.

"How did you get here? Why the hell didn't you tell me you were coming today? Why didn't Charlie call me and let me know? I'd have picked you up at the airport."

"I know you would have. But I wanted to take you by surprise. Don't ask me why. I suppose I wanted to catch you off your guard."

"You did."

"You don't mind?"

"Mind? Mind?" There was nothing he could have wanted more. "Please keep on surprising me, Sherry Valentine." Then, unable to resist another minute, he slid his hands over her slender shoulders and down her back, pulled her tightly against him, thrilling to the warmth of her body under the thin tissue of her dress. "And it's so wonderful to touch you again," he murmured into her hair.

"Ditto again," she answered softly.

Cupping her face in the palm of his hand, he kissed her softly, tenderly. She moved in even more closely, pushing into the hardness of his chest, her mouth opening under his. His pleasure exploded into passion. Just like before. No, nothing had changed. If he'd often wondered how he'd react if they ever met again, here was the answer: in the same elemental, nerve-searing, pure gut way. And here too was the same old magic.

"Sherry," he whispered.

She half-opened her eyes, and he saw everything he wanted to know. The joy at seeing him, the returned intensity. So he kissed her again. Longingly, more tenderly. Until the chilly breeze tickling a lock of hair across her flushed cheek brought him back to reality.

He laughed, embarrassed. "What a great host I am. Perhaps we could do this inside the house?"

She blinked as if coming back from a distant place. "It's so wonderfully nice kissing you. I didn't notice we were still outside."

He didn't trust himself to speak. Grabbing her two bags with one hand, he slung his other arm over her shoulder and led her into his house. Now that she really and truly was here, he certainly didn't intend to let her vanish again.

****

They sat in the main room where high windows gave out over a wooded landscape just now slipping into dusk's shadow. A log fire crackled merrily in the fireplace, right in front of the large cushioned sofa where Carston and Sherry sat side by side, but not touching. As if they both needed the space in order to think clearly. At least *she* needed the space, Sherry thought. Or else she'd never be able to keep her hands to herself.

Toying with the stem of her wine glass, she was as tightly wound as the old wooden clock ticking away steadily on the far wall. Even Carston was less at ease than he pretended. She'd seen how his hands shook when he'd taken the crystal glasses out of the antique sideboard. Was this the right time to question him? Probably not. But what time would ever be the right one? Might as well plunge in, get this over with.

"Carston? There's something I have to know. Promise me you'll tell the truth."

"All depends on the question." But his eyes

twinkled.

She shook her head. "It's about your play, *Swan Song*."

"What about it?" He stood, went over to a wooden table where the wine cooled in its bucket of ice.

She took a deep breath. "Are you sorry you asked me to play the role of Melissa? If you are, I won't hold you to it. I'll back out right away. With no hard feelings, okay? And that's a guarantee."

He came back to the sofa, carefully refilled their glasses, then sat beside her again. Only closer. Close enough to slide his arm around her shoulders. "Why would I regret choosing you for the role?"

"Because I'm not an actress, not really. You know it and I know it. I have very little experience in that domain—if you consider what I did in *Baby and the Bank* as acting experience. I'm really a performer, a plain and simple country music singer. And you know as well as I do that you're only giving me this chance because Charlie bullied you into it. Charlie's a steamroller. He could coax water rats into tuxedos." She stopped. She didn't dare look up and meet his eyes for fear of seeing how right she was. And how relieved he'd be that she'd offered to back out of the play.

There was a long silence. Sherry stared into her wine glass. She was utterly miserable.

Carston's arm left her shoulder. "Sherry, look at me, please."

She looked up, finally.

"Good," he said. "Now don't look away again. I want you to keep looking into my eyes so you'll know I'm telling the truth. That way you won't have to ask me the same question twice. And you'll never come up with something so crazy and so wrong again."

"But..."

"Listen to me. All those months ago, if you hadn't left Midville so suddenly, I'd have told you I think you're an intelligent, talented performer. That you have a very special aura when you're on stage. You're captivating, surprising, and if my hunch is right, you're a wonderful actress too."

"But you can't know that. What if..." She stopped. Carefully put her wine glass down on the low table beside her. Knotted her hands together in anguish.

"What if what?" he questioned gently.

"You wouldn't be offering me this part just so I can fall on my face, would you? As some sort of bizarre revenge. Because you think I tried to use you to become an actress."

He let out a sigh and shook his head. "Please don't throw my own stupid words back at me. If you only knew how often I've kicked myself for being such a jerk back then."

"But..."

"Stop trying to complicate things, Sherry. I don't want you to fall on your face. I'd have to be downright masochistic to want that. Why would I want to ruin my own work and make myself a laughingstock by giving the role to someone incapable of handling it?"

She smiled ruefully. Even she had to admit that it sounded completely silly. "Okay."

"Look, Sherry. You're here, in my house, so we can work together. I wrote the play, I'm directing it. Your job is to make the words and the story come alive. To make people believe in the character of Melissa. So you see? We're both on the same side." He stopped. "Is that settled now?"

She nodded dutifully, but of course nothing was settled. The worst was still in front of her: the project, her fears. And then, when the work was finished, when the play had been produced, they'd be separating again. She'd go back to her world; he'd stay here in his.

"My turn to ask a question?" Now he was the one fiddling nervously with his wine glass.

"Only fair." She smiled.

He took a deep breath. "So tell me all about Hollywood..."

"What about Hollywood? I hated being there."

"And Ned Lantini." He still wasn't looking at her.

"Ned Lantini? What about him?"

"Didn't Lantini offer you a role in his film?" he prompted. Did he actually sound jealous?

"He certainly did." Sherry smirked evilly. "He saw my acting potential right away. Topless to start with, bottomless by scene two. Not to mention the sneak previews that were supposed to take place somewhere warm, cozy, and relatively private. In his bed, for example."

"I thought you were more involved with him?"

"Involved? With Lantini?" She stopped smirking. "You have to be joking. Lantini is a complete slime."

"And what about your relationship with Jason Reel?"

Sherry gaped at him. Carston sounded like he was forcing himself to be casual. "My relationship with Jason Reel? Carston? Where did you get this information? Or shall we say misinformation?"

"Nowhere in particular. You know how gossip gets around. Actresses tell me all sorts of things."

His breeziness didn't deflect her, even for a nanosecond. "Tell me why I don't believe you. Perhaps because you're not meeting my eyes. Come on, Carston. Truth time."

"Okay. This information is in *Star*. And *Glitzy*." He looked miserable.

"*Star*! *Glitzy*?" Her mind whirled in total disbelief. "Are you joking? You're telling me you read that stuff? That you actually believe what you read there?"

He pulled himself up, desperate to retrieve some dignity. "I'd never actually read them, but I work with actresses that do."

"They do? Actresses who work in the real theater, in serious plays, actually read *Star*?"

"Some," he said miserably.

"How about Allan Mace? Didn't you read about him too?"

"What about Allan Mace?" His eyes met hers. Finally.

"Wasn't my name also linked to his in those trashy magazines?"

"Should it have been?"

"What do you think?" she challenged.

He looked at her, searching her face for information. Then smiled. And relaxed. "Just to stay on the good side of logic, if something really is going on between you and Allan Mace, would you have kissed me like you did at the door? Would you have come here to be with me?"

"No." She smiled back. "Besides, Allan Mace is too involved with the beautiful Allan Mace to even notice anyone else. We were out together in public quite often, so I suppose we can read all about it in next month's *Star*. Then we'll even find out if he asked me to marry him and if I accepted."

"Magazines like *Star* and *Glitzy* are pure, utter trash."

Sherry couldn't stifle a broad Cheshire cat grin. "But since you don't read rags like that, you wouldn't really know."

He stood, but his lips tugged into an answering, self-mocking grin. "Change of subject. Are you hungry? You must be after all that traveling. How about if I make dinner?"

"You know how to cook?"

He almost looked offended. "Of course I do."

"Don't get huffy. It's just fairly rare, you know. Men cooking."

"That's the silliest thing I've ever heard," he scoffed. "How many top chefs are men? You think women have a special gene telling them, instinctively, how to put food together?"

"Of course not. Sorry," she said contritely. "You haven't forgotten I'm a vegetarian, have you?"

"And you figure I don't know the slightest thing about vegetarian cooking."

She shrugged. "I suppose that was just about what I was thinking, yes."

"Well, I'm about to show you how wrong you are." He marched in the direction of the kitchen, and Sherry tagged along behind him. Perching herself on a high stool, she watched him pull out a deep purple eggplant, olive oil, fresh fragrant basil, tarragon, parsley, coriander, and fat yellow lemons.

"Do I have the right to ask what's on the menu?"

He nodded with satisfaction. "I don't mind

bragging. The starter is this eggplant, cooked in herbs and sprinkled with basil. After that, we'll go on to lentils and fresh spinach simmered in coconut milk with coriander, cumin, and sage. How does that sound?"

"Incredible. Where did you learn to do stuff like that? Where did you learn about vegetarian cooking?"

"In books, on the Internet. Then I just started to invent my own recipes."

"Oh," she said, her eyes still following his every move. A little suspicion had begun growing inside her head. "Since when?"

The question had come so abruptly, he didn't have time for adroit hedging. "Well...for a while now." He concentrated on slicing the eggplant into small, perfect cubes and avoided her eyes again.

"I see," she said slowly. "Since coming back from Midville, by any chance?"

"Around then, I suppose."

"Uh huh. And how long have you known I'd be coming here for dinner?"

"For a few months now." He tried, quite unsuccessfully, not to look smug.

"I see. And how could you *know* I'd accept to be in your play?"

He put his knife down on the cutting board. Met her eyes evenly. "I didn't *know* anything, okay? Let's just say I *hoped* you would."

She was stunned. Did he realize how much this confession of his revealed? Did he know how deeply involved he was? As deeply as she was, evidently. But would he admit it? Was there a chance that Carston Hewlett, loner, long-time bachelor, might be taking her seriously? She wondered.

Chapter Twelve

Clearly he was still more in control of his emotions than she was. He would be. She was absolutely, hopelessly befuddled. And lost in the feelings of desire and tenderness he evoked in her. She hardly dared meet his eyes as they set the table together, afraid he'd be able to see too clearly into her heart. See her vulnerability. She'd always been fairly lousy at dissimulation, and she knew she'd be even worse now, in these circumstances. There wasn't a nerve in her body that didn't vibrate in anticipation of what might happen when dinner was over.

Where would she be sleeping? Was there a guest room? It was impossible for her to fathom Carston's reactions. One minute there was something in his eyes...tenderness? Passion? The next minute it was gone, and mere friendliness appeared. If only she could understand what was going on. The wine she'd been drinking hadn't helped any, of course. It only added to her confusion.

Dinner by candlelight took place at the long wooden table in the main room, and despite the intensity of the situation, its newness, conversation was easy. Sherry realized she was enjoying herself immensely. On the right, the log fire crackling in the hearth sent a flickering glow across Carston's features, outlining their strength, his intelligence. Did he know how his eyes laughed when something she said amused him?

He has seduction down to a fine art, she warned herself, not that the warning would do her any good. How many women had passed through here and lost their heart in the same way she had? It wasn't a thought worth dwelling on. Not if she had her own immediate happiness at heart. Heartbreak was for later; now was for living to the full. Just a few short weeks ago, wouldn't she have given anything to be in this position?

"This meal has been absolutely wonderful," she said with utter sincerity. "If you ever decide to change careers, you'd make a wonderful chef."

"Angling for more of the same?"

"I'd be a fool if I didn't." They exchanged smiles, and the air thickened.

Then his expression became neutral again. "I'd make a rotten chef. I enjoy cooking, but I could never stand the stress of being a professional. I'm a loner, as I told you. I'd never be able to work with people around me all the time. I need this." He waved his arm, a gesture that took in the silence of the room, the still dark night outside the wide windows. "Living out here, feeling I'm alone on the planet—even though it's only an illusion."

Sherry watched him closely but said nothing. Was he trying to warn her off? Again? Tell her not to nourish any illusions as far as he was concerned? Okay. Message received.

"What about you? Will you go back to Hollywood when this is over?"

"No," she said slowly, putting down her spoon. They had just finished a very splendid dessert of fresh sliced oranges topped with the lightest cream she'd ever tasted. "Life is strange. When I did my concert in Midville, I intended it to be one of my last—my personal swan song, if you'd like. I'd been on the road for just too long, been in the public eye for so many years; I had the feeling that particular lifestyle was eating away at my soul. It was time for a change, and acting seemed like a good idea. After I got that offer in Hollywood, I jumped into the new career. And pretty soon, I realized what a bad choice I'd made."

"Meaning?"

"I want to go back to music."

"Concerts? Going on the road again?"

"Maybe," she said slowly. "I don't really know. But if I do, I'll go about it in a different way. Good-bye forever to red curls and flash. Less moving around and more research." She shrugged. "In any case, that's what I've been thinking about lately."

And since receiving his manuscript, she'd thought of other things too: what if Carston fell in love with her? What if he wanted her with him? What if this was the beginning of a long-term love story? Then what?

But thoughts like those were silly. They only paved the way to disillusion and disappointment. You couldn't survive in the big wild world if you let yourself slide into the "what if" syndrome. Carston might not let himself fall in love with her. He certainly didn't want her to stay with him forever—hadn't he just finished telling her that again? That he was a loner? That this was a short-term engagement in every way. Part two of the fling proposal made in Midville. When the play ended, they'd be saying, "Nice to have known you," and "Let's keep in touch," and "Call when you're out this way again," and "Good-bye." Unless their relationship could continue on some less committed level. One that had them living close to each other but not together. She thought of those pretty wooden houses in the nearby town of Cutter's Edge...Then cut the thought short.

Why was she so besotted with this man? So ready to make any concession just to be near him? She had to pull herself together.

"You look exhausted," said Carston, gently.

She looked up, nodded. He was right. It had been a long day, an incredibly stressful one. It had become stressful again. In a different way. "I am," she said simply.

He stood. Came around to behind her chair and began, very gently but wonderfully, massaging her shoulders. She closed her eyes. It felt fabulous. Every time he touched her, it felt fabulous. It was the same magic that was working now, just as it had a few months ago. It hadn't gone away, changed, or lessened. She sighed.

He misinterpreted the sound. "Come on. Bedtime."

Whatever that meant. She stood, tried to sound casual. "I suppose we'd better tackle the dishes first."

"Certainly not. Mrs. Ried comes down from the village at the crack of dawn every morning. She'll be astounded to find out I have a house guest, especially a house guest as famous as Sherry Valentine."

He slipped his arm around her shoulders, led her away from the table. It felt so good to be here, close to him, nestled in the warmth of his body. How lucky she was to have the chance to be with him again.

"I bet your Mrs. Ried has already heard the news

from every single person in Cutter's Edge. I had to go into a grocery store and ask for directions to your house, and the snoopy woman in there asked me right out if I was your 'friend.' If Cutter's Edge is anything like Dog's Pass, the news was ricocheting around the community before my left foot was back in the taxi."

Grabbing her bags, he led her down a stairway. "The bedrooms are all on a lower level and lead out onto a beautiful wildflower-covered prairie. You'll see it in the morning, and I'm willing to bet nothing in Dog's Pass can beat it."

"I'm inclined to agree with you," said Sherry. Not that she'd tell him why. Not at this point in the game. Besides, was this the time for another long explanation? No. But it never seemed like the right time. Especially since she was always lost in those heady sensations whenever he was close: the loving feeling, longing, desire. She wanted nothing more than his arms around her tonight, his lips against hers, his warmth beside her, his scent floating around her. She wanted so much to make love with him. If she didn't have that…

"Carston?"

He stopped, looked down at her, his eyes unreadable.

"Do I get to sleep with you?"

"Is that what you want?" His voice was husky.

"More than you can imagine." She wanted to kick herself. And what if he said no? And she'd promised herself she wouldn't make a fool of herself, wouldn't come on strong.

He put her bags down on the floor. "More than I can imagine? Are you serious? I just wasn't certain…" He sighed. "I mean, this is my house, and you're in my play. We'll be working together, and I didn't want you to feel that...I mean...I wanted to be a gentleman..."

She didn't let him finish. Turning to face him, she stood on tiptoe, planted a soft butterfly kiss on his wonderful lips. Feathered them. Felt how right the contact was.

He sighed, a ragged sound of want. And suddenly the air crackled with the strange electricity they generated together. Folding his arms around her, he kissed her tenderly, then more deeply.

Kisses? She couldn't remember any kisses being like this. His tongue explored her mouth, and she arched against him, her hands clutching the cloth of his shirt, fires raging deep in her belly. From a great distance, she heard herself moan, heard his ragged breath mirroring her need. Then, abruptly, he swept her into his arms like weightless warm air, carried her through a doorway.

Incandescent moonlight touched white walls and a large bed in the center of the room. And gently, as if she were made of porcelain, he slipped her fine cotton dress over her head, unclasped the lacy bra revealing breasts swollen with desire, slid her thin panties down over her hips.

He stared at her, his eyes feasting in her nudity. "How beautiful you are," he said, his voice low in his throat. "So much beauty, and all of it's for me." With the tips of his fingers, he traced her face, her mouth with utmost tenderness. Then bent, drew each achingly sensitive nipple into his mouth, teasing it with his tongue. Continued downward in a burning path, over her belly to the hot, damp juncture of her thighs.

Coils of passion ricocheted through her. "Please

wait," she gasped. "Please, Carston. I want to see you naked, too. Please."

He laughed, a rich, throaty sound. "Please?" His eyes glittered.

Slowly he undressed, and she took in the taut chest, his long, strong legs, the hard maleness showing how much he desired her. He was totally naked now, and she stepped in closer. Caressed his body with hers, reveled in the tight strength of his muscles against her softness.

"You're the one who's beautiful," she murmured, curling one leg around his hip, so that her intimacy touched his. His ragged moan of pleasure delighted her. "I want you so," she whispered. "I want to explore you with my fingers, with my tongue, with my whole body." She moved downward, tracing a moist pathway from his taut male nipples down to his flat stomach.

"Wait," he gasped.

She looked up at him, saw his blazing eyes.

"I want this to go slowly," he growled. "Just this time. This first time." He pulled her up into his arms again. "I've waited so long…"

And so had she. It had been an eternity, all that time separating them. Now, the waiting was over, and she wanted him to know how much he meant to her. That she was here because he mattered to her. Very much. She hesitated, only for a split second, before opening her heart. "I love you. I do love you, Carston Hewlett."

"I know," he whispered.

"You know?"

He leaned back slightly to look at her. Cupped her chin lovingly. "Thank you."

He hadn't said he loved her too, but that didn't

matter. She'd read his face, and everything had been written there. He felt the same about her, she knew that. He loved her. He wouldn't admit it, he couldn't. Not yet. But there was no mistaking his care, his trust, and his tenderness. Those were wonderful things, and they were enough for the moment. She could wait for the words. They'd come later.

****

This wasn't California sunlight dancing across the pillow and love-tossed sheets, and she hadn't imagined the night spent with Carston either. A whole night of wonderful, satisfying lovemaking, drifting to sleep in his arms, waking again to his kisses and more loving. Instinctively, her hand reached out, searched for him.

He wasn't there. Her eyes shot open and she sat bolt upright. Where was he? What had gone wrong?

Then she saw him, coming back through the doorway carrying two cups of what smelled like coffee. He was stark naked. And unutterably wonderful-looking. Already her fingers tingled with the desire to touch. Their eyes locked and the air in the space separating them vibrated. Carefully, he put the cups down on a dresser top, then sat down on the bed and pulled her effortlessly into his arms.

"Good morning, Sherry," he said softly, his mouth against hers.

When they broke apart, she read pure tenderness in his face. And vulnerability also?

Then, without warning, his expression changed, became something more controlled. He reached for the coffee cups, handed her one. "Milk, no sugar. Just the way you like it."

She stared. "How do you know that?"

"Traverton," he said shortly. "Breakfast in the Paradise Café."

"You remember?" She was astounded. It had meant that much to him? It must have.

He looked embarrassed. "Just my writer's memory coming into play. Keeps all the banalities of daily life carefully filed away for some future use."

That was only an excuse. He was covering up again. Concealing his feelings. But she knew what she'd read in his face only a brief minute before. That tenderness he felt he had to hide. Why? Was he warning her not to read too much into this situation? Possibly.

The hell with warnings. How did he know where this would go? He wasn't a fortune-teller and neither was she. She would play this relationship for all it was worth. Without defenses. And, if it eventually came to a rocky end, then she *still* would have gained something. An experience. Better forget about the heartbreak for the moment.

With a gentle fingertip, he brushed back a strand of hair from her forehead. "You ready to start work on the play this morning?"

Anxiety shot back into the picture again, dragging along with it a fear of failure and timidity. "Look, Carston. I still don't know why you're insisting on having me in your play. Why not get someone great for the role of Melissa? Someone like Lila Patterson. I saw what she could do on stage. She's great. Experienced. Talented. She would do the role justice."

"You ever hear Lila sing?" His voice was dry; his mouth twitched into a grin. "*Swan Song* is about a singer, right? A singer at the end of her career."

165

"That's a lousy argument. The part is written for an actress."

"Sherry, tell me what you think of the play. Have you read it yet?"

"Is that supposed to be a bad joke?" She was miffed. "How banal and ungrateful do you think I am? And don't start treating me with condescension again, Hewlett. Of course I read it. I devoured it. I pretty well know the whole thing by heart already."

"You do?" He looked astounded, almost doubtful, as if he didn't dare believe her.

Embarrassed, she waved her hands in a dismissing gesture. "Well, that's not such a big deal for me, you know. I've been learning song lyrics ever since I was around four years old."

But now he was pleased as well as surprised, she could see that—although he was doing his very best to hide it. "Do you like the character of Melissa?"

"Oh, I really do. She's so independent, so strong, yet so touching. I love the whole play, Carston. Very much. I just don't know if I can carry it off."

He shook his head. "Too late now. No exit possible. You're here, I'm here. Work starts right after breakfast."

"Too late? Why? Because...well, because of last night...You don't have to..." She stopped because he looked annoyed.

Then annoyance vanished. He stared at her speculatively. "I think, finally, I know what the real problem is. You're frightened, right?"

"Scared silly." She nodded with relief that he finally understood.

"Okay then. Let's put this into perspective. This

production is for the theater festival in Brandt. I'm not hard-heartedly pushing you out onto the New York stage, right? This is a chance for you to find your feet. There's no pressure, and there will be no horrible consequences. Now, how do you feel about it?"

"Still scared," she said honestly. "But I'll work on it, okay?"

"Hollywood didn't scare you?"

"Scare me?" She stared at him in disbelief. "You can't even imagine the scripts I read out there. I was even offered a role in a film about teenage Egyptian mummies who come to life again after a nuclear disaster. The mummies end up eating any human survivors."

Carston began to laugh. "If that's all it takes to give you confidence, I'll write a mummy scene into the play."

"Go ahead. Make fun of me." She sniffed, tossed her head. And hoped her lucky star hadn't shifted off into some very distant, unattainable galaxy.

****

She was sitting out on the terrace, perfectly unaware he was watching her, admiring the shine of her soft pale hair escaping from its loose chignon and the glint of a sunbeam on her cheekbone. He felt a wave of tenderness rolling through his soul, and he wondered if he would ever get tired of touching Sherry, of looking at her and being with her.

She still didn't know he'd thought of her night and day while writing *Swan Song*. That she'd been his muse. That his fear of losing her completely had spurred him on. Inspired him. Made him do everything in his power to get her back. Of course he couldn't have given the role of Melissa to anyone else: this was Sherry's play. But if he told her that, wouldn't it put more pressure on her? He couldn't take that risk. Her fear of failure was too strong.

Or perhaps he hadn't confided in her because he wanted to hide how much he cared? Did he even want to admit it to himself? Sure, she was here with him now, but hadn't she said she wanted to return to her singing career? And that meant, after this play went on the stage at the Brandt Festival, the relationship would be over. Sherry would be gone; he'd go back to his normal, solitary life.

The thought didn't give him much pleasure. So what did he want? Permanence? Was permanence even a possibility after living alone for so long? He was almost certain it wasn't. Not at his age.

How would she feel about living out here in the country? She'd grown up in the backwoods and probably had no desire to return to the country life. She needed bright lights, applause, and adulation.

How could they stay together? She'd be on the road for much of the time, and he'd have to read gossip magazines to find out what was going on. What about the paparazzi? He could just picture a squadron of journalist's cars lining the road in front of his house and fans sneaking through the woods. Goodbye to peace, quiet, and a private life.

All things considered, it was better to wait, play for time, and not let his heart open totally. Or futilely. And why even worry? How much time had he now actually spent with Sherry? A few days? And here he was, fretting about a future they'd probably never share.

Chapter Thirteen

Carston had gone into the village for supplies. She was alone in the house, going over the written notes he'd left with her. They'd been loving and living together for two weeks now. And working steadily on the play. Now Sherry understood what acting entailed, the commitment, the hard work, and the deep satisfaction. But the panic was still there, of course, and the fear of failure, even though she told herself over and over again that this would only be a theater festival presentation. If she really *did* fail, there would be no dire consequences and no international shame.

But *Swan Song* really was an exciting play, with its intimate, changing moments, the depth of Melissa's character. Even if Carston was a demanding director—and that he certainly was—he was also intelligent and compassionate. Carston. Just thinking about him made her heart turn over. She'd loved him before; now, being with him day in and day out, her feelings had grown even stronger.

The telephone rang. Sherry looked up. He hadn't bothered to put on the answering machine. Should she answer? Carston had never told her she shouldn't, and Sherry knew very well that he received calls from other women—she could tell from the tone of his voice. For business calls, he was impersonal, professional, dominant. For personal calls, he was companionable, communicative, and reserved—but that was when talking to men. Talking to women, his tone was deeper, smoother. A voice that could charm snakes out of their hidey holes. Not that she eavesdropped. Sometimes she just couldn't help over-hearing...Couldn't stop the tiny stabs of jealousy either.

The telephone jangled for the sixth time. Sighing, Sherry stood, stalked over to the thing. Her hand hovered, just a fraction of a second, before lifting the receiver. What was there to hide? She was here, in Carston's house, for a perfectly legitimate reason. Who cared about the steamy nights, sensual mornings, and glorious passion they shared?

"Hello?"

There was a fleeting but very perceptible pause at the other end of the line. "Perhaps I have the wrong number?" The voice was breathy, feminine.

"I very much doubt that," Sherry said dryly. Then promised to try and sound less caustic.

"I'm trying to reach Carston Hewlett."

"Of course you are. He'll be back any minute now. Do you want to leave a message?"

"Ah—" There was a long pause. "No. I'll call back." The owner of the breathy, sexy voice hung up.

"And what is it *you* have to hide," Sherry said sourly. Then with derision, stuck her tongue out at the dead receiver.

"What's my telephone done to offend you?"

Sherry whirled. Carston stood in the doorway, laughing at her. Damn it. Why did he have to look so gorgeous? Her jealousy evaporated. Why worry? She was the woman in Carston's house—and bed—at the moment. That was one advantage the mysterious caller didn't have.

She went to him, curling her arms around his neck, letting her fingers slide into his wiry hair, fitting her body tightly to his. His eyes darkened and, lowering his head, he took her mouth with a fierce, possessive passion. When they finally broke apart, they stared at each other, hearts thumping.

"I'm glad I don't go out shopping more often," he said huskily. "We'd never get any work done."

"You're even a worse taskmaster than Charlie Bacon."

He quirked an eyebrow. "Is that a compliment or an insult?"

"Your interpretation." Her forefinger lazily traced the beautiful line of his mouth. "By the way, you had an anonymous phone call."

"Is that why you were pulling faces?" He chuckled. "How anonymous?"

"A whispery, sexy female anonymous caller. When I asked if she wanted to leave a message, she hung up. Perhaps I shouldn't have answered your phone?"

"Why shouldn't you have?"

"Just in case any of my rivals are on the line." She tossed her head and forced herself to look arch.

"You don't have any rivals," he said softly. So softly she almost didn't catch the words.

"I don't?" she asked breathlessly.

The telephone rang again, a horrid jangling noise. Damn the awful machine, ringing at all the wrong moments. And that particular moment had been shifting toward absolute perfection.

This time Carston handed the receiver to her. There was no sexy whisper. "How's tricks, chicken?" Charlie

Bacon's over-hearty, eardrum-splitting bark came through loud and clear.

"Fine, just fine," said Sherry as coolly as possible. She didn't really want Charlie to know how far her relationship with Carston had gone. She was somehow afraid that, just by talking about it, it would somehow be jinxed. She knew Charlie didn't trust Carston. Maybe he didn't even like the idea of her being here in his house—aside from the fact that Carston's play would enhance her reputation. She also knew Charlie would do his best to protect her from heartbreak—although she didn't want his protection. She'd gone into this with her eyes open. "But I'm being worked like a slave."

"Good to hear it. Hewlett taking good care of you at least?"

"Wonderful. You should see the things he feeds me. He's a man who knows the way to a woman's heart is through her stomach."

"That certainly puts another light on how effective he is as a slave driver," said Charlie with his habitual, evil chuckle. "There's a little tidbit of information I have for you, by the way."

"Let it roll."

"If you decide to go back to being a singer when this is over, I can line up concerts all across the country. People are calling me all the time, wondering what you're coming up with next."

"Concerts? I'll think about it. But I'm warning you, Charlie, no more orange hair, no more traveling around on the star circuit. I want to get away from the popular aspect of music. Go more deeply into its roots. Help people learn. And don't start telling me that it won't be a money-maker. I don't care."

"We'll see," Charlie said, placating instead of argumentative.

"See what?"

"Just rattling away, chicken. Nothing important."

When she put down the receiver, she was convinced Charlie was hiding something. He was as subtle as a hippopotamus sliding down a mud bank. So what was up?

"You feel like shirking work this afternoon?" Carston asked.

Sherry looked up at him from under her lashes. "To do what? Something wonderfully sexy?"

"Go for a walk," he answered simply.

"A walk?" Her eyes widened with surprise.

"Don't you like walks anymore? You did back in Traverton." He felt disappointed.

She grinned openly now. "Of course I still like walks. I've liked them ever since we were stuck up on that mountain together. You told me back then that you loved walking too, but since I've been here, you haven't proposed one, not even once."

It turned him into mush, her reaction, and he wondered why this was so important to him. "You think you could handle several miles through the valley?"

"Several miles?" She sniffed, tossed her head. "I'll show you the stuff I'm made of, Mr. Ivy League Hewlett. Back in the old days, down in Dog's Pass, we had to walk twenty-five miles every night just rounding up the gophers for milking."

"You have walking boots?"

"Yeah. Right. I needed a lot of those in Hollywood."

"Okay. You'll have to borrow a pair of mine. And wear two or three pairs of socks to fill them out."

"Won't I just look like a princess?"

Probably will, he thought.

They took the narrow, damp trail leading out of his own land and down toward the meandering Cutter River. Carston loved being outdoors, loved the freshness of the air, the beauty of his surroundings, the feeling of freedom the country gave him.

When they reached the bottom of the valley, Sherry sat down abruptly on the riverbank. "Thank goodness." She was panting.

"Thank goodness for what?"

"That we're too fast for whatever's coming after us."

He was ashamed of himself. "I'm sorry. I guess I was pushing it a little. I'm so used to walking on my own, I forgot my pace couldn't possibly be yours." Even if her legs were long, his were more muscular, stronger, and used to this terrain.

"You try waddling around in boots three sizes too big."

He looked down, sheepishly contemplated the boots that on her looked Goliath size. "We'll have to go shopping. Get you your own pair." Which meant this wouldn't be their last walk together. *But is it worth buying a pair of boots for the little remaining time she'll be here?* "Let's follow the river. The going will be easier."

"Don't mind if it isn't," said Sherry. Closing her eyes, she took a deep breath. "Actually, I'm having the most wonderful time. If only you knew how often I dreamt of doing just this when I was back in

Hollywood. Maybe a million? No, more than that. Each time I found myself trapped beside another over-sized free-form swimming pool in the middle of a manicured garden, cocktail in hand, forced to listen to the latest trendy music group."

He tried not to feel too delighted. "Yes, trapped. That's how I've always felt about the frills that go with success."

Sherry's arms opened wide, embracing the fields, the valley and the entire horizon. "Out here, all I can hear is the wind rustling and the river bubbling. At night, I love falling asleep to the sound of hooting owls and rubbing branches. And in the morning, the birds are always singing their hearts out. It's wonderful. It's perfect. It's ideal."

How much he'd hoped she would see the beauty that was so important to him. But her enthusiasm could be momentary. "We can be snowed in for weeks during the winter. Sometimes there are power cuts, and that means no heating aside from the open fire, and no lights except for petrol lamps. That would probably drive you crazy."

"Me? Are you kidding? Sounds like heaven. Or like being cozy, warm, and safe inside an enchanted castle with lots and lots of lovely books to read."

He sat down on the bank beside her, not caring if the ground was still moist and chilly at this time of the year. He was feeling extremely grateful to her; he was infinitely touched. Too touched to even speak. He reached for her hand, curled her fingers around his.

"Anybody else live out this way?" she asked softly. "Or are we the only creatures around?"

He managed to find his voice again. To sound

perfectly normal. "Actually, the area is less abandoned than it seems. I have some very nice neighbors. So nice, they and their farm stay hidden just behind the line of trees over there." He pointed to a nearby ridge.

"Mama Bear, Papa Bear, and Baby Bear?"

"No." He grinned. "The Plummers. Goldie and Ned."

"This has to be a joke, Hewlett. She's really called Goldie? As in Goldilocks?"

"No joke. If you feel like walking that far, I can guarantee Goldie makes the best pear pie in the whole world."

"Got tired of all that porridge, huh? Serves her right for mooching."

The wet grass underfoot tugged at their boots, and the path narrowed. Carston watched Sherry out of the corner of his eye. No, she wasn't pretending. She really was enjoying herself, taking in her surroundings as if the experience of being in the country was entirely new to her. And again, the strange doubting thoughts—the sort he'd had several times over the last few weeks— niggled at him. There was something she was hiding, he was sure of it. Something about her life story didn't quite fit. He didn't know why he felt that way, and she hadn't said anything. He just felt it in his bones.

He stopped abruptly. Pointed to the ground. "Look, Sherry. Bacon and eggs."

"Bacon and eggs?" She looked down, then back up at him, puzzled. "Is too much fresh air making you strange and unpredictable? Bacon and eggs, you said?"

"I did." He watched her with growing curiosity. "Don't you see?"

"See?" She looked at the pointing finger, looked

down again. "Bacon and eggs," she repeated. "Is there a clue to help me decipher this mysterious code? Because you're pointing to a few straggly weeds and some spring flowers. Come on, Carston. Be a sweetheart, and let me in on the joke."

He knelt, gently touched a tiny yellow flower tinged with red. "Bacon and eggs—that's what this flower's called. Didn't you know? When these come up, it's a sure sign summer is on the way."

"Oh."

"And that. Over there." He pointed again. "You know what that is?"

She stared. "Looks like pointy spinach to me." Then nodded, raised her chin, defiantly. "Okay. Got it. This is a test. And I'm failing badly, right?"

"It's called rabbit's ears," he told her gently. "Do you know what it's good for?"

She shook her head. "Tell me."

"Skin infections. Burns. It's a wonder plant. Edible too."

"Okay. Fine." She shrugged. "Well, if a plant doesn't come in a pot surrounded by wrapping paper and pretty ribbons, I'm out of my depth." She pointed to another shaggy, spiky-looking clump. "Tell me what those are."

"Stinging nettles. Nasty to touch, but great stuff for homemade soup, or for steaming and eating like spinach. Nettles are also a natural fertilizer, an insecticide, and the unique food source for certain types of butterfly larva."

Sherry's eyes narrowed. "They teach all about making soup out of nasty weeds in Ivy League schools?"

Carston quirked an eyebrow. Shrugged. "Beats me."

"If anyone knows, you should," she retorted.

He was finding it hard to hide his amusement. "And tell me why I would?"

"Because that's your background, isn't it?"

"So you've told me."

"Oh." She shook her head slowly, looked faintly confused. "It really isn't?"

"And you don't know much about plants and grasses, do you?"

"Not a lot," she acknowledged.

"Especially not for a country girl."

She only stared at him, wordlessly. And defiantly.

"Come on, Sherry." He smiled, took her hand in his. "If we stay here much longer, we'll start sprouting moss."

****

As the Plummer's farmhouse came into sight, Sherry felt more than relieved. Her feet were feeling as though chipmunks had been gnawing at them for hours. Images of hot coffee and pear pie swam before her eyes like a foretaste of nirvana. But when they entered into the courtyard of the farm, she instantly divined nirvana was unreachable. At least, this afternoon it was. A young, anguished girl of around thirteen rushed out to meet them.

"Oh, Carston. I've never been so happy to see anyone in my life. I'm alone, and I don't know what to do. Mom and Dad have gone into Barston, and I can't reach them. I telephoned you, but you weren't there. I also called Mr. Tourup, the vet, but he's out somewhere and I'm scared crazy."

"Just tell me what's wrong, Penny."

"It's Mrs. Brown. She's having her piglets. She's already had eight, but she's pounding around like she's in pain."

"Certainly sounds awful," muttered Sherry. "Poor Mrs. Brown has my sympathy, whoever she is."

Carston threw her an amused look over his left shoulder. "Mrs. Brown just happens to be a sow."

"Well, thank heaven for that." Sherry still couldn't see why Penny Plummer was happy to see Carston under these circumstances. What was a playwright going to know about pigs? Unless any old drama at all was good grist for his literary mill.

"Let's go take a look at the poor lady. We'll see what we can do for her." His smile was relaxed and comforting.

The situation was getting stranger and stranger. Sherry trailed after Penny and Carston as they entered a warm, dark barn. And saw that Mrs. Brown was certainly a sow—no one in the world could have denied that. A very large sow. Enormous, in fact. Sherry had never been this close to a pig in her life, and she was astounded. She'd always imagined them as small, pink, slightly fuzzy, and most probably reasonably cuddly. Mrs. Brown was long, hugely fat, bristly, and she stared at the human intruders with small, malevolent eyes. The last thing that interested her was a round of cuddling.

A screeching throng of pale newborn piglets writhed around Mrs. Brown, trying desperately to reach her teats, but Mrs. Brown wanted nothing to do with the lot of them. Instead, she stormed furiously in circles and emitted strange groaning noises.

Sherry shrank back against the barn wall

179

fearfully—something that didn't escape Carston's notice. His eyes fairly glowed with undisguised amusement.

"You know anything about pigs?" he asked her.

She shook her head. Then Mrs. Brown yowled, and veered in her direction. Deftly sidestepping, Sherry fought down a feeling of panic. She'd just caught sight of something sharp-looking and yellowish in the creature's mouth. "I didn't even know they had teeth," she moaned. "I just thought pigs sort of gummed at things."

"They don't." Carston's voice was dry. "Pigs can give you a nasty bite. Stay away from her, Sherry. She's in pain, and she doesn't know you. But I'm still going to need your help."

"You are?" The situation was getting worse by the second.

"The first thing we have to do is gain her confidence."

"Pleased to meet you, ma'am." Sherry forced a weak smile.

"Penny, go get a bucket of clean, warm water and a blanket. We'll have to keep the piglets warm. Sherry, your job will be to keep them covered up and all together. Otherwise there's a risk of Mrs. Brown squashing them as she moves around. Be careful of their teeth too. Baby pigs are born with really sharp ones."

"Like cute little vampires," Sherry muttered. By the time Penny returned, Sherry, with Carston's help, had managed to herd the squealing, squirming babies over to one corner of the stall. Now she covered them with the blanket and tried to keep them in place. At the same time she didn't let Carston out of her sight, not even for one second. She watched as he knelt down in the straw, all the while talking to big fat Mrs. Brown. The sow watched him suspiciously. Then, probably because there was no choice, she made the decision to trust him. Coming nearer, still grunting with pain, she lay down in the straw.

"That's a good girl," said Carston stroking her gently.

"You certainly do have a way with women," Sherry jibed from her corner. But she was fascinated. "What's wrong with her anyway?"

"She obviously has a least one other baby inside of her. Pigs are very long animals, and the piglets are sort of lined up inside in two rows. Now that she's at the end of her labor, she just doesn't have enough strength to give birth to the last one or two—if they're still alive. I'll have to go in with my hand and help her out."

"Just like that?"

"It's not easy. In fact, it could be downright painful for me. Pigs have very strong contractions."

Sherry held her breath and watched. After a rather hard and tense struggle, Carston finally pulled the last baby out of the sow. It was wet, bloody, bedraggled, and weak. But still very much alive.

Mrs. Brown grunted and again Carston stroked her flank. "There. You see. She's nice and calm now. Sherry, you can let her have her babies back."

"Okay, kids, go for it." Sherry urged the babies out of the corner, watched them scramble wildly around their mother, looking for their first taste of warm milk. Then she stared at Carston as he washed up in the bucket of warm water Penny had brought. He had a lot of explaining to do, she decided. She'd obviously made a few mistakes about the man.

****

Night was starting to fall, and the damp sweet smell of the fields enveloped them as they wended their way home.

"Okay. True confession time. How do you know all about pigs? And flowers."

Carston shrugged. "Because, quite simply, I grew up on a farm not fifty miles away from here."

"What about your Ivy League background?"

"That's what I was hinting at earlier. There isn't any Ivy League background. I went to the local school, and when class let out in the afternoon, I helped my father with the chores. I can tell you all you want to know about cattle and fodder."

"I thought you were a terrible snob when I first met you at the radio station."

"I know," he admitted ruefully. "But you made me realize the error of my ways pretty quickly. There I was, trying to give off the image of a sophisticated New York playwright, and I was suddenly confronted by the sexiest, brightest singer I'd ever met. And she came from the country too. From Dog's Pass. A place so tiny, no one in the world has ever heard of it, or can even find it on a map. I figured if I didn't watch my step, we'd be chatting about the soybean harvest in no time flat."

"Hmph." It wasn't much of a comment, of course, but she knew it was her time to say something.

"Of course, I was wrong, wasn't I?" he persisted.

She didn't answer. Just stared down at the dark, muddy track as if concentrating on where to put her feet.

He stopped, gently took her arm, turned her around to face him, cupping her chin in his hand so she couldn't look away. "Tell me, Sherry."

"About what?" she asked, keeping her voice light to deflect his curiosity.

But he was insistent. "You don't really come from the country, do you? Dog's Pass is a myth."

She took a deep breath. "That's not true. Dog's Pass is a real place, I swear it is. It just isn't where I said it was."

"In the Ozarks? That's what everyone's told, right?"

She was silent for a few seconds. "Actually, Dog's Pass is quite far from the Ozarks."

"How far?"

"Really far. About a thousand miles or so, in fact. It's, uh, well...Dog's Pass is in the Bronx."

"You come from the Bronx?" He would have been slightly less surprised if she'd said she'd recently flown in from Neptune.

"You see? The Bronx doesn't sound very authentic for a country singer. In one minute you're going to start laughing at me, right?"

"I promise I won't." He hoped it was dark enough for her to miss the twitching of his lips. "What did you do with your Bronx accent?"

"Traded it in for a country twang. No big deal, of course. Being a singer is all about having a good ear."

"Okay. I'll buy that. Now, what about the rest of the story?"

"The rest of it's almost all true. Almost. Dog's Pass was what everyone called the derelict gas station about fifty yards away from the home. That's where I used to play. When I could sneak out."

"The home?"

"That's right. The home. The orphanage. The bit about my mother is all made up too."

"The mother who didn't really care about you?"

Even in the night, her eyes were defiant. "She really didn't, you can believe that. I was dumped off on the steps of an abandoned grocery store when I was around one. No name, no papers, no family, no background. Just another cast off, anonymous kid. That's why I started lying about my mother when I was little. Seemed to me a mother who didn't care was better than having no mother at all. Or a mother who'd had a baby, then got so bored with it after twelve months or so, she'd left it on the street."

"And that's why becoming a star was important to you," Carston said slowly.

She nodded. "Of course. I figured if I could make almost everyone in the whole world love me, then I'd somehow be showing the parents who didn't want me how worthy I was. But there's a good side to the story too: the need to be loved gave me the strength to fight to the top." She stared at him defiantly for a minute. Then defiance melted. "It all sounds silly now, doesn't it? Keeping my real background a secret. Not ever talking about it. Inventing something that never existed."

"No. It doesn't sound silly." He pulled Sherry into his arms and held her tightly. "It sounds healthy and strong. You were a kid who took a bad situation, then invented something positive. You fought and won." His hand smoothed her soft, warm hair.

"You're the first person I've ever told the truth to, you know. Not even Charlie knows."

"Good," he said gently. "The truth is always the best way to create a solid base."

Chapter Fourteen

"Nothing to fear but fear itself," muttered Sherry as she stared at her colorless face in the mirror and winced. If she were any paler, she'd be transparent. She clasped her hands in her lap to stop them from trembling. "All your fault," she said to her image. "If you hadn't gotten that crazy idea in your head about being an actress, you wouldn't be in this position. Why did you wait until this late in life for a career change? This should teach you a lesson." The words didn't make her feel one iota better.

Oh, help. In a very little while, she'd be out there with what would seem like a million eyes staring at her, and all of them would be waiting for her to fail. What if she tripped, fell on her face when she walked on stage? What if she forgot her lines? Her mind raced trying to remember the nuances in the manuscript, the movements, the gestures she'd gone over, so often, with Carston. And, with a sinking heart, she realized her mind had gone absolutely, perfectly blank. She couldn't remember her first line; she couldn't even remember what the play, *Swan Song*, was about.

"Stop worrying. Think of something else. Something nice."

She tried. She thought of last night. A candlelit dinner. Again. Everything she and Carston did together was always so damned romantic. And sexy. And good.

Of course, last night she'd also been a nervous wreck and hadn't really enjoyed either the dinner or the candlelight, but her nervousness had been nothing compared to what it was now. Strangely enough, Carston had only been amused at her fears. Worse, he didn't even appear to take them seriously.

"You realize that your reputation is shot if I mess up your play. You'll be a laughingstock."

"Sherry, you're not going to mess up my play. You've been going on stage for years. Why are you so nervous? I'm not."

His arm around her shoulders had been warm and comforting—or it should have been. Deep inside, Sherry didn't believe for one single second that Carston would forgive her if she didn't do his work justice. How could he? Surely his disappointment would destroy any trust that had grown up between them. And how would she be able to face him at the end of the play?

At least Charlie was out there in the audience, sitting beside Carston, watching. Good old Charlie would rescue her if she messed things up too badly. He'd cart her off stage, drag her far off to some never-never land. To a forgotten cave in the mountains where she could hide out until the whole world stopped rolling around, sneering and howling at her failure. Until Carston stopped searching the world's surface with a basket of rotten eggs in his hand.

And amongst all those people out there in the audience, Sherry knew there was one woman who certainly wouldn't be a well-wisher. A woman who'd be more than happy to see her fall on her face. Just as she'd gone into her dressing room with Thelma the

187

makeup artist, Sherry had seen Carston talking to a tall, very elegant, beautiful woman. One with violet eyes: Lila Patterson. Lila Patterson would be a witness to her failure. How she would sneer about her to Carston.

What the hell was Lila doing here anyway? For the moment, Sherry didn't have the strength to think about the implications of that woman's presence. It would be something she'd deal with later—after the disaster.

There was a knock on the door, and Thelma marched in, ready to check on her star. "Well, stand up," she ordered briskly. "Let's have a look at you."

Sherry stood, feeling sick.

"Nervous, are you, dear?" Thelma smiled, tucked a strand of Sherry's hair into her low chignon.

What was there to smile about? "Scared out of my mind," Sherry admitted weakly.

"Well, that's just the usual stage fright. Every performer in the whole world gets it. Believe me, I've seen it over and over. Musicians have it, conductors, public speakers, actors, and actresses. It doesn't matter if you're a professional or an amateur: stage fright is a fact of life. Don't you ever have it before a concert?"

"Of course I do. But this is different. I know what I can do as a singer. This is my first acting experience."

Thelma smiled. "You know what they say, don't you?"

"Nope. I don't know much of anything anymore."

"If you have stage fright, that means you'll do a great job. It's the ones who take it all in their stride, the ones who think they're perfect, who don't do well out there. You need to be nervous in order to be good. Sarah Bernardt once said, 'Stage fright only comes when you have talent.'"

Sherry smiled faintly. "You've almost convinced me. But I bet the world is chock full of really rotten performers who have stage fright too."

Shaking her head, Thelma adjusted the collar of Sherry's simple blouse. "Because they don't know how to take nervous energy and put it into their performance. You do. I've seen you on stage and you give yourself to the audience like a gift. That's probably why Carston believes in you. You'll be fine."

Sherry looked at herself in the mirror again. This was also the first time she'd be appearing on stage without the gaudy disguise she'd affected for so long. Perhaps all those fringes and sparkles, that thick makeup, the orange hair had given her courage? Perhaps she'd always felt that the real Sherry had been hidden by a mask and was, therefore, protected.

"How long now?"

"Four minutes." Thelma left the room.

Four minutes. Time enough for something extraordinary to happen, something that would get her out of this awful situation. A meteorite could hit the theater. Giant killer ants could charge into the dressing room, kidnap her, and carry her off to one of their colonies. She waited. But the minutes ticked by relentlessly without jaw-clacking *Formicidae* coming to the rescue. "Where are those guys when you really need them?" she muttered.

The door opened. "Stage right, Sherry." Nick, the stage manager, gave her a big wink. "Break a leg, kid."

In the wings, she heard the hum of the audience on the other side of the curtain. Her heart was pounding furiously. Thirty seconds to go. What was her first line? Her mind reeled: she couldn't remember! She really *had* forgotten absolutely everything. She had to get out of here, run away. Fast. Her eyes searched desperately for an opening. A trap door. A long vine she could shinny up.

The lights dimmed. The audience stopped chatting. Now there was only deathly silence. It was starting. The play was starting, and she still couldn't remember one word.

Slowly the curtain rose. *Too late to escape now.* All eyes were on her as she entered. The blinding stage lights became even brighter. *My first words. What are my first words?* She didn't know…

"It started on Monday." Yes, that was her own voice she was hearing. "A Monday, just like any other. In October." Those were her opening lines. The right ones.

And then she forgot she was Sherry Valentine, that Sherry Valentine existed. She'd become Melissa. A singer whose career had come to an end.

****

The play was over, and the audience was cheering. The curtain came up for the fourth time, and the applause still didn't diminish. Carston. Where was Carston? He should be out here with her. He was the one who should have the glory. It had been his words, his brilliance that had carried off the play.

Here he was now. Striding out of the wings, carrying a bouquet of flowers—perfect red roses—that he handed to her. Red roses? Then clasping her free hand in his, they bowed together, and the audience cheered more loudly. The moment was sublime.

The curtain came down for the last time, and for a few brief seconds, they were alone in the world. Just the two of them. His eyes were filled with such tenderness.

"Thank you," he said softly. "I'm so proud of you."

"Thank you," she answered. What else could she say? Her heart was too full to speak. And oh, how she loved him.

Then there were people surging around them, shouting their congratulations. Two journalists began firing questions. At her, and at Carston. Cameras flashed.

"Chicken. You were great! I knew you could do it, sweetheart. I knew it!" Charlie's fat red face beamed. Just before he could grab her and hug her soundly, Thelma reappeared from somewhere and quickly rescued the bouquet of roses.

Sherry felt as though she were emerging from a dream. She didn't have an ounce of fight left in her. Someone else was hugging her now. "You did it, Sherry. You did it." The voice was surprisingly familiar.

"Allan Mace. What in heaven's name are you doing here in Brandt?"

"You didn't really think I'd miss Sherry Valentine's theater debut, did you?"

"Oh, Allan, I'm so touched. It's absolutely wonderful to see your gorgeous face again." It was. What she'd thought was a very superficial Hollywood friendship had obviously been far deeper than she'd known. She fought desperately not to burst into tears.

Allan noticed, of course. He smirked. "You *should* be touched. Coming here was a terrible sacrifice. Just look what the climate's done to my hair."

Banality can be a wonderful thing, she thought. The urge to cry vanished.

191

"Sherry, darling," said Allan. "Tell me. That glorious, tall, violet-eyed female beside Hewlett, that's Lila Patterson, isn't it?"

Sherry followed his stare and her happiness diminished radically. "Yes, that's Lila Patterson, all right." Who else in the world had violet eyes? Who else would be beside Carston, as if that were the most natural place in the world for her to be?

"You know her?"

"In a way." She was forcing herself to sound normal, but the feelings of resentment and jealousy were hard to control. She had to admit it: Lila and Carston looked wonderful together. They made a lovely pair. She'd always known they would.

And Carston had already forgotten that she, Sherry, even existed. He'd allowed her to be in his play. He'd let Charlie talk him into giving her a break. But had he talked her into his bed? No. She'd been the one to do that. Now she had no one to blame for this situation but herself.

And who had mentioned love? She had. He hadn't, not even once, touched on the subject. He'd never said he felt more than friendship for her. She'd been the one who'd fallen head over heels in love with him, a confirmed bachelor. The sexiest man she'd ever met. And the most unattainable.

Had he been amused by her declarations? No. She knew Carston too well now. He was no egotistical maniac. He was a kind, warm man. A generous one. He'd probably been pained by her devotion, her love, because he knew he was unable to return it. Love was a gift he didn't want, hadn't asked for. Now that the play was finished, their temporary relationship was over. It was good-bye. Back to old loves.

She saw Lila whisper something in Carston's ear, and he laughed. Yes, he looked perfectly, blissfully happy. Just the way he should be, thought Sherry, bitterly. His play was a raving success; a beautiful woman was at his side.

She had only one choice: she had to get out of there. Do it with dignity. Show Carston she knew she had no hold on him. That she wouldn't hang around, beg him to love her, be a nuisance. She wouldn't kick and scream now that the door was closing. She'd had the honor of working with a brilliant, talented man, and to show how much she appreciated what he'd done for her, she'd give him back his freedom. *No muss, no fuss.* He'd be mighty relieved.

Allan wasn't paying attention to her anymore: he was having a very earnest conversation with a journalist, promoting the famous Allan Mace. Carston and Lila were deep in private conversation. Charlie had vanished—had probably gone off to smoke one of his stinking cigars. No one, absolutely no one, was watching her at the moment. So, the time was right.

Good-bye, to all of this. She wanted no flashing cameras to capture her defeat. She wanted no headlines. As slowly, as casually as she could possibly manage, she turned, walked toward the wings. She'd sneak back to her dressing room, grab her purse, and make a run for it. *Just move slowly*, she told herself. *Slowly, slowly so no one notices.*

She couldn't leave through the main door, of course. The lobby would be blocked by people: journalists, those in charge of the festival, people from the audience. And a crowd was clumped around the stage door too. Was there another way out?

In the dressing room, she rolled her jeans and sweater into a bundle, stuffed them into her tote, and slung her handbag over her shoulder. Then she peeked into the corridor. Not a soul around. Stealthily, quietly, she headed in the direction of backstage. There had to be a fire exit somewhere past the wilderness of electrical wires, abandoned sets, stacked furniture. Another long corridor on the left was perfectly dark, empty. Would there be a door? Sliding her hand along the wall, she managed to keep her bearings.

Then she heard a noise behind her: a click. A door opening and closing? She couldn't be certain. She stopped, stood still. This was definitely not a comforting place to be lurking in. *Just the right setting for a chance encounter with the Phantom of the Opera*, she thought miserably.

She inched forward. Again she heard something. Stopped. She wasn't alone, she knew that now. Someone else was here. Someone—or something—was coming up behind her. She could feel, but not see a presence.

In the split second before she whirled around to confront whatever it was, a massive hand clamped onto her arm with the tenacity of a Doberman's jaw.

"Where the hell do you think you're going?"

She almost sank to the floor with both relief and dismay. "Charlie."

"Spill the beans, chicken." She couldn't see him, but his voice was mirthless. Uncompromising.

It put her on the defensive. "Don't you dare manhandle me." She struggled to free her arm.

"Who's manhandling you?"

"You are. Let go of my arm."

"What were you doing? Sneaking out?"

"Not sneaking. No way was I sneaking. Just making a quiet, unobtrusive exit, that's all."

"Oh yeah? Well, let me just roll out a few facts to you."

"Don't bother," she spit out.

"Fact is, this is your party, chicken. You're the star. People are waiting for you out in the lobby, and they want to congratulate you, meet you. There's champagne. And journalists. And festival organizers. And where the hell are you? Creeping out the back door, leaving Carston looking like a jerk."

"Guess what else. I'm not creeping, not sneaking. I'm walking. And you've got it all wrong. I'm not the star here. Carston is. I'm just the person who was in his play. The one who spoke the words he wrote down. The talent belongs to him, right? Now will you let go of my arm?"

"Excuse my being nosy for a minute—"

"What do you mean, for a minute? You've been nosy for a whole lifetime. Let go of my arm, Charlie Bacon."

"Answer my question first."

"Let go of my arm or I'll scream."

"Scream away. How are things between you and Hewlett?"

"What things? Let go of my arm. Now!"

"You love him, right? Back in Los Angeles you told me you did."

"All right. Yes. So what? Everyone makes mistakes."

"Why's it a mistake?" He released his grip.

"What's wrong?"

"Just go back in there and take a look. Then you'll see what's wrong."

"Got it." Charlie emitted a rasping sound that sounded, annoyingly, like laughter. "Lila Patterson. So that's it. Carston was talking to Lila Patterson, and you're jealous."

"Don't *you* sound smug." Then she gave up the fight. Her shoulders sagged. "Okay. Yes, I am. I'm wildly jealous. So what? But the point is, I don't want Carston to think he's obliged to me for anything. We had a wonderful time together. It was brilliant working with him; I had the honor of being in one of his plays. But now he'll want to get on with his own life. And I want to keep my last bit of pride."

"Carston's not allowed to talk to other women?"

"Stop making me sound silly. Lila Patterson isn't just any woman. We went down this old road back in Midville, remember? Lila and Carston make the cutest couple I've ever seen. I'd also like to remind you that *you* were the one who warned me off Carston. *You* told me to stay away from him."

"Sure. But that was before."

"Wasn't it just! Before you bullied him into putting me in his play." Before she'd woken up beside Carston every morning, seen his face across the breakfast table, felt his touch at night. Before she'd learned to love their complicity, their incredible lovemaking, his intelligence, and his kindness.

"What the hell are you talking about?" Charlie roared.

"Don't bother denying it. Carston would have given the role of Melissa to Lila or some other wonderful actress, but you forced his hand. You're aggressive and insensitive. You push people around until they can't think straight." She felt horribly close to crying again. She knew she was being unjust to Charlie. If only her heart wasn't aching so badly.

"Sherry? Didn't he tell you?"

"Didn't he tell me what? And what didn't who tell me?" The hell with sounding intelligent.

"Carston. About the play. I wasn't supposed to let the secret out. I gave my word. I guess it doesn't matter now, though."

"What secret?"

"I didn't bully him into giving you the part, chicken. He was the one who contacted me. He thought you might refuse if he asked you directly. He wanted you for the role because he wrote this play just for you. To tempt you away from Hollywood. I didn't even want to accept, at first. I thought you'd get hurt again."

"What?"

"That's all there is to it. He knew he'd messed things up back in Midville, and he wanted another chance to get to know you better. To be with you. What better way to do that than write a play for you?"

"How do you know all this?" It sounded so hard to believe. But hope was growing.

"Because Carston told me, that's how. We've become good buddies—telephone buddies. He even came all the way to Memphis to see me, convince me he really cares about you. So I admit I was wrong about the guy. I like him." Charlie put his hand on Sherry's shoulder. "Stop acting like a wounded toughie. If you love him, go get him. You've always fought for what you wanted in life. Why stop now?"

"What if he doesn't love me?" she asked weakly.

"Are you joking? Everybody loves you. Haven't you noticed the way he looks at you? The way he talks to you? Come on, chicken."

Sherry could only stare into the dark, lost for words.

"But that's not the whole story." Charlie was suddenly sounding very sly. "If tonight's success is anything to judge by, this play's going places. Boston, New York…London. Just think, chicken."

Suspicion reared its head. "Okay. I get it. The voice of Charlie-manipulator's coming through loud and clear."

"So? Actresses need managers just like singers do. It'll be a nice change for me, getting in with the Ivy League culture crowd. No more cowboy gear. Just tuxedos and silk underwear."

****

"Where the hell have you been? I've been searching all over for you." Carston was wildly furious. He'd gone through ten minutes of panic when he'd realized Sherry had vanished. "What do you think you're playing at?" His hand clamped, vise-like, around her arm.

"Charlie just did that to me," she said dreamily.

"Charlie did what?"

"Put a vise on my arm. It didn't feel the same way when Charlie did it, of course. It was minus the sexy electricity."

He stared down at her. She met his gaze evenly, and her lips curved upwards with the seductive little smile that always turned him into pussycat. He loosened his grip. "Where have you been?"

"Actually, I was running away," she said nonchalantly.

"Running away?" His heart was pounding so loudly, he thought folks in far-off Cincinnati could hear it. Then he shook his head. "Well, you don't seem to be very good at it. You didn't get far."

"Don't you dare make fun of me."

"I'm not." Strangely enough, he only felt like smiling too. "Believe me, I'm taking this very seriously. Why were you running away?"

"Because I thought you didn't love me. But you do, don't you?"

"Of course I do," he said, his voice thick with emotion. "I love you very much. I've been in love with you ever since I met you at the radio station. But so what? Where's it going to get me? Or you. Or us. I can't ask you to spend the rest of your life in Cutter's Edge."

"You can't?"

"It's really a very dull place."

"Mm-m-m." She grinned lasciviously.

"And I spend hours every single day locked up, writing."

"I noticed."

"And you've always lived in the fast lane, in the limelight, surrounded by people. It just doesn't seem like the right combination."

"Didn't you ever think of asking me what I thought?"

He sighed. Closed his eyes, rubbed them with his fingers. Then looked at her again. "No. I guess I didn't. But you're right. I should have."

"But?"

"Fear of rejection, I suppose. I'm just a simple country boy, at heart."

"Fine." She nodded. Looked up at him, her heart full. "Could you just say it again? That bit about loving me very much?"

He laughed softly. "I love you, Sherry Valentine. And I'm sorry it's taken me so long to come out and say it. Forgive me."

"I love you, Carston Hewlett. I promise it will never be dull living with you. It's all I want. I hate cities, and I love Cutter's Edge. I love everyday life with you; I love the way the countryside smells; I love walks; I love sticky mud. I could even get to love that piggy Mrs. Brown, if she'll accept my advances."

"Then you'll stay with me?" he asked quietly.

"Forever, if you want. Besides, you did promise me a pair of walking boots. You think I'll let you get out of that?"

He didn't care who was watching. Pulling her into his arms, he gave her the most wonderful kiss.

It was all the journalists needed. Cameras clicked wildly.

"I can just see the headlines in *Star*," Carston growled.

"SHERRY VALENTINE CHANGES HER MIND YET AGAIN
IS IT FOR REAL THIS TIME?"

Sherry pulled back slightly. Smirked. "But of course you don't read *Star*. Or do you?"

"I'm deeper and more complex than you imagine." He hoped he sounded mysterious.

A word about the author...

Born in New York, raised in Toronto, J. Arlene Culiner has spent most of her life in England, Germany, Turkey, Greece, Hungary, and the Sahara. She now resides in a 400-year-old former inn in a French village of no real interest. Much to everyone's dismay, she protects all living creatures—especially spiders and snakes—and her wild (or wildlife) garden is a classified butterfly and bird reserve.

Visit her at:

http://www.j-areneculiner.com